Praise for *Growing Up on Route 66,* the first novel in this series:

"Lund presents an entertaining story of small town life - paperboys, the gentle aspects of life in a simpler time and the wonder of the people who make small towns the linchpin of America. Through the eyes of Mark Landon we find that the answers to the myriad questions of life and love aren't always easy to find."

--Bob Moore, ROUTE 66 MAGAZINE (Volume 9, Number 1; Winter 2001-02)

"If the trials of Kevin, Paul, and Winnie on the television show *The Wonder Years* remind you of your childhood, you'll enjoy this coming-of-age book. The author grew up in Rolla, and his characters, Mark Landon and Marcia Terrell, live in a small Missouri town along Route 66. The narrator tells funny stories of adolescence in the 1950s. As an adult, the narrator has a philosophical outlook. 'The road I've traveled has clearer landmarks when I look behind me than when I was moving forward,'"

--Tricia Mosser, MISSOURI LIFE (Volume 29, Number 6, December 2001)

Praise for *Route 66 Kids:*

"Babyboomers coming of age in a small Midwestern town on Route 66. It's a decade later but it reads like the 'Summer of '42.' An extremely heartwarming and nostalgic look at young people's angst during this age of wonder."

--ROUTE 66 FEDERATION NEWS (Volume 9, Number 2; Spring, 2003)

"*Route 66 Kids*, follows the fortunes of his earlier hero and heroine of *Growing up on Route 66* , Mark Landon and Marcia Terrell, taking them through high school to the eve of Mark's departure for college at Southwest Missouri State College and Marcia's departure for ... but you'll have to read the book to find out where Marcia is headed ... . No matter how often you've heard the phrase/title *You Can't Go Home Again*, Michael Lund's book convinces us that Thomas Wolfe was wrong. You can go home again, and *Route 66 Kids* takes us home wherever home was."

--William Frank, FARMVILLE (VA) HERALD, May 31,2002.

Praise for A Left-Hander on Route 66:

"[*Left-hander*] is a howl with just enough of the serious to add contrast and spice."

--William Hoffman, award-winning author of *Godfires, Tidewater Blood,* and many more

Praise for Route 66 Spring:

"... highly recommended for anyone seeking an absorbing story of life in the Missouri Ozarks, peopled not by the archtypical Hillbilly, but by Lund's characters who bring this fascinating and beautiful part of the country to life."

--ROUTE 66 MAGAZINE, Vol. 12, No. 4 (Fall 2005)

Praise for Route 66 to Vietnam: A Draftee's Story:

--"an engaging tale that flashes back to the narrator's Vietnam War tour.

--THE VVA VETERAN, January/February)

--"able to reach that place so many of us seek within ourselves."

--ROUTE 66 MAGAZINE, Spring 2005 (Volume 12/Number 2)

Praise for Michael Lund's Route 66 Novel series:

"I finished your [first] novel ... and was struck by how perfectly it seemed to encircle (of course) the world of childhood and its heady veering toward adulthood. It's a loving and funny book ... and made me recall with mingled pleasure and embarrassment all the twinges and itches and passions of adolescence. Well done, and thank you for putting it into my hands."

--Carrie Brown, author of *Lamb In Love* and *The Hatbox Baby* "wonderfully well-wrought [first] novel, set in a place that's still the stuff of myth, about coming of age in a simpler time when sex was giddily mysterious and life was filled with endless possibilities."

--Bernard Edelman, editor of Dear America: Letters Home from Vietnam and Centenarians: The Story of the 20th Century by the Americans Who Lived It

"In *Growing up on Route 66*, Michael Lund gives us a loving look through the telescope of memory, resurrecting forgotten feelings in the idiom of adolescence sharpened by the lens of age and wisdom. He takes us back to a time when the road ahead was a winding one, just right for joyrides, meant to be wandered, with curious roadside attractions and shady stops along the way. Reading [his] book is like returning to a summer night when you were young, when life was full of promise, mystery, and terror, that time at twilight, before your mother called you in to wash up and go to bed, when you were playing a leisurely game of kick-the-can and wished that the game could just go on and on. Fortunately, Lund promises that it will go on, in the second book in his series, *Route 66 Kids*, and, I hope, many more to come."

--Eric Kraft, author of The Personal History, Adventures, Experiences & Observations of Peter Leroy

Route 66 Chapel

By

Michael Lund

BeachHouse Books

Chesterfield, Missouri, USA

Copyright

Graphics Credits:

Cover painting by Joy Boettcher Utzinger. Cover design and graphics by John Lund.

Publication date 2006

ISBN 1-59630-012-4 Regular print BeachHouse Books Edition

ISBN 1-59630-013-2 large print (16pt) MacroPrintBooks Edition

First Printing, 2006

Library of Congress Cataloging-in-Publication Data
Lund, Michael, 1945-
  Route 66 Chapel / by Michael Lund.
      p. cm.
  ISBN 1-59630-012-4 (alk. paper)
  1. United States Highway 66--Fiction. 2. City and town life--Fiction. 3. Chapels--Fiction.
  4. Historic buildings--Fiction. I. Title.
  PS3562.U486R678 2006
  813'.54--dc22

                              2006022214

www.beachhousebooks.com

an Imprint of
Science & Humanities Press
PO Box 7151
Chesterfield, MO 63006-7151
(636) 394-4950
www.beachhousebooks.com

Route 66 Chapel

Michael Lund

For Ethel Woodruff Macy.

ACKNOWLEDGMENTS

In writing about religion, even the unorthodox doctrine of Route 66 Chapel, I'm reluctant to acknowledge the guidance of any specific person as I'm pretty sure he or she would, at some point in this narrative, wince at the sloppiness of my representations of spirituality. Still, I wish to thank the priests, ministers, chaplains, and laypersons who have strengthened my faith over the years, especially my maternal grandmother to whom the book is dedicated.

Jim Shifflett edited and proofread the final manuscript, and his precision and care are greatly appreciated. I also need to thank Dr. Robert May for spotting a significant number of errors while reading a late draft. Once more I must express my gratitude to Dr. Bud Banis for his ongoing support of my writing and for the larger mission he has undertaken with Science & Humanities Press. I am proud to be associated with his work.

As always, any errors in fact or inconsistencies of narration in the pages that follow are attributable solely to the author.

Michael Lund

Prologue: the Lady or the Tiger

Thirty years ago, my husband stole the story of birth, traditionally a mother's property. Now I'm going to take it back.

Accounts of childbirth belong to women, after all, because we are the central players in that event. Men have been kept out of--or chose to keep out of--the maternity ward. So grandmothers told mothers who told daughters the secrets of labor, the miracle of new life.

My first pregnancy, however, came in the 1970s, a time of social change. Men had begun taking La Maze classes in the weeks preceding the trip to the hospital; they donned masks to coach their wives through delivery; and they put on rubber gloves in the delivery room to receive the child right out of the mother's womb.

Mark took advantage of this new approach to an ancient rite to establish his story of pregnancy and birth. He has used it for years to challenge those feminine accounts which so often take over social gatherings of married couples. I accepted his insertion of a masculine voice into such girl talk--until now. No doubt, Mark will come to resent this repossession.

The truth is, I was out cold at the climactic moment of Nelson's delivery and have only a partial narrative of my own to offer. But I must cross the line into the father's experience in order to prepare you for the chapters to follow. In that story of choices--the lady or the tiger--I hope to break down the sometimes tragic barrier between ourselves and others.

We had no clue throughout the nine months of Nelson's gestation that his birth would be anything but normal. When the time came, however, just minutes after my arrival at the hospital, an alert nurse noticed unusual rhythm in the fetal heartbeat. My obstetrician, called in promptly, acknowledged sufficient signs of stress to recommend an immediate Caesarian.

The cord had wrapped around Nelson's neck, and he would not have survived a natural birth. Now past thirty, healthy and the father of two, our son's destiny is not the subject of this story. In just a moment, I'll move beyond Mark's small moment of crisis to, for me, an uncharacteristic project in storytelling.

All alone in the traditional "New Father's Courtesy Room," Mark waited several hours to hear the result of the operation.

"After all the training we'd done," he explains, "I felt like I'd fallen back in time. This was the kind of place where my father waited for word that I was being born, as his father had paced before him." If there are women listening, they'll often cluck in real or mock sympathy: "Poor guy!"

"Maybe I'm really not liberated, after all," Mark continues, "but one of those throwbacks, a unregenerate chauvinist."

He's baiting his audience, of course. Those who've heard the story before (like our children) roll their eyes, a sign to others.

"So there I am, hour after hour, all alone, not knowing."

It isn't hours and hours, of course, as Dr. Lincoln, taking no chances with me or Nelson, proceeds swiftly with the Caesarian.

"Is the love of my life OK? Is my child-to-be safe? In those primitive days, we didn't even know the sex ahead of time!"

He'd been reassured by the doctor and several nurses that there was little danger to me or the baby, the problem having been spotted so early. But Mark wants the drama to build.

"Finally, I can't stand it in the waiting room. Every old issue of *Life* magazine has been read cover to cover. I'm on my second time through the Bible--well, the Old Testament, at least."

Some of us know *Life* was no longer a regular weekly then. And the Bible detail usually causes even gullible listeners to suspect that Mark has begun to lace his tale with hyperbole.

"I start pacing the hall, back and forth in front of the elevator. I figure Doc will reappear here with the announcement. Finally, the little arrow above the elevator doors that points to the floor number begins a descent from 5 to 4, from 3 to 2--ding! Dr. Lincoln, poker-faced, emerges."

Rather than linger on the doctor's report, Mark moves quickly past that good news (a healthy boy!) to concentrate on an unanticipated dilemma he faces next. This skipping over my and Nelson's condition is often disconcerting, especially to women.

"Doc tells me I can come with her to the third floor. I follow into the elevator, relieved to find that all is well. When we step off on that floor, though, I find my trials are just beginning."

He always pauses here to generate suspense, but the crisis toward which he's been building is really not confined to the hospital setting. What he reveals concerns another step in that prolonged transition between childhood and adulthood, between being a son and becoming a father.

"When we come out of the elevator, Dr. Lincoln, who stands beside me, waves her hand to the left and says, 'Your wife is down the hall in 213. It's a private room; you can see her now.'"

Again, listeners feel temporary relief.

"If only she'd stopped there, though!" Mark continues. "I would have known what to do. I would have turned left, marched down the hall, entered room 213. This was a direct, clear, meaningful course of action." His audience can only nod.

"But then Dr. Lincoln waves her other hand to the right!" Mark waves his hand now as well. "'Your son is in the maternity ward at this end of the hall.' I can see the large glass windows on the other side of which, it is certain, Nelson Landon, only hours old, rests in his little bassinet. He's surely all alone, since there were no other pre-fathers with me earlier."

Most listeners see no problem here; the story has a happy ending. But Mark insists that he's in an untenable position.

"OK, my friends, what am I supposed to do--go left to my wife, the mother of my child, who needs my love and support? Or go right to the family heir, who also demands my love and concern? I can't, you see, go both directions at once! And whichever way I turn, I abandon someone to whom I owe total allegiance."

He will bask in his listeners' sympathy now as long as he can get away with it, though he knows--and everyone in his family knows--the resolution is swift and precise.

Dr. Lincoln sees his hesitation and, a hand on his shoulder, pushes him gently toward the room where I lie in a semiconscious state and says, "You go to your wife; I'll bring your son to you both."

And there it is: a neat solution, courtesy of sensitive and wise Dr. Abigail Lincoln.

What Mark doesn't see is how his perception of this problem reveals something larger, a habit I consider characteristic of him, his generation, and his region of the country. He sees every choice as being between the lady and the tiger.

Mark could be husband *or* father in this situation, he thinks, not both. To become one is to deny the other. So much for him, and for others like him, is either/or, left or right, yes or no, on/off. Behind one door is a tiger; behind the other is a lady.

Yet, surely this is not so. We are all in this world young (to our parents) and old (to children); we have both public and private identities; we are good and bad. We don't have only two doors to open. Sometimes we choose not to open either.

I believe the story I'm about to tell is peculiar to a region and to a generation--the Midwest and the children of the Cold War; but I suspect it applies in quite a few other contexts as well. Shortly, we'll see the principle of either/or embodied in one of the 1950s favorite symbols, the famous highway, Route 66. Such norms enabled great accomplishments like the Mother Road, but they also created unrecognized restrictions, boundaries for travel.

Mark, one of that group of either/or believers, appears here, as I say, to introduce the dilemma of others you will meet shortly. And I, a Southerner of the same age, but shaped by different forces, hope to be the outside observer who can depict their struggle objectively. As I see it, even their favorite symbol, Route 66, is made up of opposites: east- and westbound lanes. "America's Main Street" is one road. Its traffic just goes in two directions.

Now, how did I, a counselor by profession, come to be recounting this tale instead of some experienced, award-winning author, one of NPR's famous voices, or an investigative television reporter? Well, after many months working with one special group I've been inspired to--and they've approved--an attempt at presenting their story. (Of course, I've changed the names and some details, preserving client confidentiality.)

"Route 66 Chapel" is about opposing choices. But it's also about the joining of opposites. I'm convinced that men, who don't give birth, and women, who do, can form unions that renew the human spirit. While people take contradictory positions in what follows, their tales come together at the end into a single story. I can only hope it's a good story, and that I tell it well.

Bel Landon

St. Louis, Missouri

Volume One: Marital Status
Chapter I: Wishy-Washy

Pulling up the shade on her store's front door and turning the sign hanging there from "Open" (for her) to "Closed" (customers now see the opposite), Norma White reminds herself of the moment America started to go bad: December 31, 1963. That was the day, she knows, when the first Route 66 bypass around Fairfield opened. Norma can see direct decline from that event to the recent decision to demolish Route 66 Chapel, despite the campaign launched by Molly Smith to save it.

Anybody, claims Norma, could have seen that 1963 road around Fairfield was all wrong, if they'd been paying attention. True, her own attention wasn't where it should have been that day, and for one pretty obvious reason: Robbie Burns' backside. Three years in a row she'd been watching him bend over a football and rise up in her adolescent fantasies.

And my goodness, what a good-looking boy Robbie was, Norma thinks nearly four decades later. Over six feet tall, a clean crewcut, big strong hands. He snapped that pigskin to Jimmy Whittier and then smacked into the other team's biggest player. Norma had been ready for him to put her on her back, too--only, of course, after the appropriate preliminaries of those conservative days: courtship, engagement, church wedding.

There were other reasons she wasn't paying attention to the Route 66 ceremony out by the Banner Hotel forty years ago. Eighteen and intent on starting out on her own, she had no idea that anything President Eisenhower had proposed (interstate highways) and the town fathers later accepted (a by-pass) would affect her life. So that intersection on the edge of town was hardly a place she felt she should keep a watch on.

Norma later moved Robbie from her imagination into her love life, just in time for their senior prom in the late spring. They dated until he went off in the fall to the College of the Ozarks. In two years, the plan was, he would take over his daddy's hardware store. She wasn't going to college herself, and Norma told Robbie she would wait for him to finish. If he made the grades first semester, she conceded, he could do then what he was always begging to do--"park his car in her garage."

Unfortunately, Robbie got to do that exactly once, as an enthusiastic Army recruiter got hold of him down there in Branson and convinced him to quit school early. Robbie was lost in some Southeast Asian jungle, perhaps thinking of Norma. But therein, she knew, lay another example of what went wrong with America in the 1960s: the young started dying instead of the old.

Norma will tell anyone who'll listen--especially her new friends, Jennifer and Gene Grey, at the bakery--that you could see it in the three-lane cement road curving north around town just past the high hill on which the Banner Hotel rested. The new extra-wide road split off from the old highway and wound three and a half miles through some rough hills. It rejoined "Business Route 66" west of town, on a long descent off the Fairfield Plateau heading toward the Gasconade River bottom.

"It's that reversible middle lane I'm talking about," Norma insists, "a violation of logic, if ever there was one!"

Cars could go either way in that center lane. Eastbound traffic, wanting to pass, used it when no one was coming from the other direction. Then westbound drivers would take over the same space in the next minute to get around cars in front of them. But, Norma tells the Greys, "traffic lanes should be one way or the other--east or west, north or south, this way or that."

To her, this three-lane Route 66 was part of something larger and more pernicious: everything started to be reversible at that time. Up switched with down, left was also right; round pegs got jammed into square holes. And it happened on a grand scale: the Cold War was frosty one minute, red hot the next (farewell, Robbie Burns!). Women dressed like ladies today, but put on pants and neckties tomorrow. Men grew hair so long they sported pony tails, then shaved their heads like monks. Today, an abandoned but still drivable stretch of three-lane Route 66 out in the county stands in Norma's mind as a reminder of the beginning of the end.

"Thank goodness," Norma tells her friends now, "I can take a stand against wishy-washy, a few of us diehards in Fairfield insisting that right is right." She pauses. "Wrong is also wrong, and, as Molly says, Route 66 Chapel must be preserved."

If Norma had known they were going to change all the rules, she would have sold out and headed for the big city way back when Robbie was killed. But she continued the full-time job in Miller's Knit and Fit Shop she had taken after graduation.

Downtown on Eighth Street, that store enjoyed a prime location. Elderly Miss Minnie, a spinster, had been good to Norma, letting her work Saturdays the last two years of high school. Norma confessed her dream, to succeed Minnie as shop owner--after, of course, many years of devoted assistantship.

In December Mayor Paterson was telling all the dignitaries gathered at the Banner Hotel that this new road would begin an era of regional development. But Norma came to believe that the new route for America's most famous highway, the "Mother Road," was exactly what they called it at first--a "by-pass." It took a double-crossing path around town, leaving locals out of the loop.

Of course, people like Norma naively believed in the continued prosperity they'd enjoyed since the war. (The good times the new Mayor Paterson anticipates are, she fears, even more illusory.) Back then, babyboomers were packing the schools and bringing business to local merchants. New homes sprang up, additional stores opened on Main Street, Sputnik's success brought investment to science and technology, which fueled expansion at the four-year state school located in Fairfield. People were continuing to "get their kicks on Route 66."

Even Norma's now longtime foe, Harry Blackburn at the Heal-All Shoe Shop, had bought into that fool's notion that everyone could live happily ever after. He was sticking it out longer than she was, even though (another reversal!) grownups now wear sneakers that won't take new soles or replacement heels.

They want Norma to sell her store, one of the oldest buildings in town and--because of the redecorating Minnie had done in the 1950s--a fine example of Fairfield's distinctive style of interior design. She suspects they plan to do something like gentrify the neighborhood, turning the old shoe factory into condominiums (an artificial form of housing, in her opinion: a factory is for production, not living).

They've ruined what's left of downtown anyway, she thinks, gazing at the block of empty buildings across from her. The Greys' bakery is hanging on around the corner, but Norma doesn't understand how in the world those two young people are surviving.

Norma used to have out-of-town customers in addition to her local clientele. Old Route 66 (the proper, two-lane version!) passed one half-block from her store. Folks staying at the Stony Court would spot the sign out front and wander up, often after eating at The DC, the town's famous roadside diner. (All this before the downtown hotels turned into edge-of-town motels.)

Maybe she should have seen it coming when Robbie kept wanting to play football with her. In hindsight, she realizes this was a sign she should have studied more closely than his hind end!

"You hike and do a buttonhook," he'd say. They might be in the park near their neighborhood, Fairfield Gardens.

"Girls don't play football," she told him. "We throw funny."

In those days that was true, though now they say it was more cultural than anatomical. Female hips are hung differently than male hips--for reasons of childbearing--but elbows and shoulders are not. Women didn't throw well because their parents put dolls and knitting needles in their hands to train them for other tasks. Norma says her parents were doing the right thing.

"You don't have to throw," Robbie insisted. "I'm the quarterback. You just hike and go out for the pass."

"You're a center, Robbie. You don't throw the ball."

"Come on, good-looking. Down, set, hut-hut-hut."

She knew what he really wanted: to get his hands on her while she was reaching over for the football. And he wanted to tackle Norma later, wrapping her up in those big, strong arms of his. She didn't mind, as he wouldn't try to go too far in a public park like this. There were little kids on the swings not too far away, watched by a pair of mothers.

Still, she didn't want to play football for another reason, an early suspicion, generated by the situation, that unpleasant changes were on the way. She feels now that she was glimpsing another shadowy sign of a wishy-washy world emerging. You see, for all his size, his strength, and his skills as a football lineman, Robbie Burns threw just like a girl.

Now, the woman who loved him then wants to hold onto his memory and the past in the form of a little church off what has become known as America's Highway, Route 66 Chapel.

II: Heaven and Hell

"'I think,'" Molly Montgomery whispered to her boyfriend nearly forty years ago, "'I think I'm a little bit pregnant.'" She meant, of course, she might be a few weeks pregnant.

She's addressing now the senior women, plus one young friend, who constitute a support group in this small Midwestern town. They giggle at long lost innocence, Molly's and their own.

The teenagers of the past, Molly and Jerry Smith, were at the movies that Saturday night, a place they went before necking in the Smith family DeSoto down a lane off Old Farm Road.

"What?" Jerry asked a little too loudly, spitting an unpopped kernel of popcorn back into the box he had tipped up just a moment earlier. While he was only seventeen and she a year younger, they both should have known there is no such thing as "a little bit" pregnant: you either are or you aren't.

"Shhhh. It's probably a false alarm anyway." She put a hand on his arm and looked nervously around her. Fortunately, everyone else in the theater seemed intent on watching a spectacularly forgettable Western, *Dead or Alive, Cowboy and Indian*.

But it wasn't a false alarm. Molly knew it already, and, many decades later, she feels the pregnancy inside her even as she speaks to her senior friends. Having been as regular as clockwork since the age of twelve, she'd missed the period after she and Jerry got carried away in the back seat of the DeSoto.

"Who knew?" she tells Norma White and the others gathered in her living room this winter evening. "Who knew how quickly you could move from pleasant petting to his climax inside you?" They all laugh again, this time nervously. Most are thankful this crisis is in the distant past and that American mores have changed even in this conservative community.

"We were just babes in the wood in those days," Norma admits. "Not a clue about how to avoid being eaten by wolves."

"Things are different now," insists Claire, the most forgiving in the circle. "That's the way it was then, but those days are over. I take our present over that past."

There is a murmur of agreement, countered by a grunt from Norma, before Molly resumes her story.

Because of her condition, Molly knew her immediate future would veer off dramatically from the trajectory of her classmates'. No final year in the Latin Club; at an end the regular clarinet practices for pep band; goodbye to senior play and senior prom. She would have to hide her growing middle in loose clothes until the end of the school year. In those days, pregnant girls were expelled, even if married.

"I remember how it was done," Claire adds. "The girl walks carrying her books out in front, at arms' length, resting on her stomach so it doesn't seem to be a baby poking out there. But it's more than a chubby tummy, and she can't disguise it forever."

Molly says she felt her parents would agree to a quiet wedding, perhaps kept secret until summer. "But I didn't know what Jerry would do."

"Ah," say her listeners, a collective sigh of recognition at the nature of the male animal. (Each will, however, admit in private to at least one exception.)

Molly explains that she and Jerry had dated on and off for several months, but he was not her declared "steady." He might, she knew perfectly well, insist he wasn't "the one," even though there had been no "other." Many in Fairfield knew Mitch Robinson had played that trick on Debbie Anderson two years earlier. Debbie then spent a summer and fall with a cousin she had never mentioned to any of her friends in some other state. Most understood that a baby was given up for adoption.

Once the initial shock of possibility had sunk in with Jerry, Molly planned to explain that her suspicions of being pregnant had proven correct. A week after their movie date he promised to meet her in what would become Route 66 Chapel. Maybe in a house of God, she reasoned, he'd live up to his responsibility.

This tiny stone church, in the style they call Ozark Giraffe, sat on a quiet street in a quiet neighborhood. Once on the edge of town, the back of its long thin lot later lay along the current version of "America's Highway." Membership had dwindled to a handful of stooped Fairfieldians whose eclectic set of beliefs seemed contradictory to anyone outside their circle.

If you'd asked in the 1950s how many religions were represented in this town, you'd be told there were two: Protestant and Catholic. But those extremes were oddly blended in Blessed Union Gospel Chapel. Vaguely Protestant in liturgy, the church still allowed Mary, the mother of Jesus, a special place in its iconology. And perhaps that's why Molly Montgomery chose it for this meeting that would shape the rest of her life.

The congregation had always insisted on leaving church doors unlocked, despite robberies and vandalism elsewhere. There was not much of value to steal, they argued, and some saw the one-room building as a sanctuary. Perhaps wandering hoboes slept there overnight, watched by the Holy Mother. Runaway children might hide inside long enough to realize they wanted to go home. Even students at the state college could just need a quiet place to pray before exams. Molly expected, though, that she and Jerry would be alone for the meeting that would decide her future.

Molly's been prompted to tell her story so many years after the fact because there's talk of demolishing the old church, called in recent years (because of its location) Route 66 Chapel. It became town property after the last of its members passed away, but no other denomination has showed an interest in purchasing it. Molly wants her friends--her very good friends--to know how important the little stone church is to her. They all have their own reasons for trying to save Route 66 Chapel.

"I probably shouldn't have made Jerry that ultimatum, but in those days, we were told over and over about the 'saved' and the 'damned.' I didn't know if I'd be lost if we got married, but I knew for sure I would be if we didn't. So I put it to him that way: either we were married and saved together, or we were each damned apart. It was a choice of heaven or hell."

Jennie Grey takes such a sharp intake of breath that they all turn to her. The youngest woman here, she blushes. "I'm sorry," she says. "It just seems so harsh, so final. To me at least."

"Now, now," Claire pats her arm. "It's OK. Like we said, people feel differently now."

Norma snorts. She believes society has lost all standards, though she's not quite sure what should be done in such a case.

"The story does have a happy ending, of course," Molly continues brightly, as she rises and starts to collect coffee cups and the little plates on which she had served cookies and slices of pound cake. "In that wonderful little chapel, my Jerry went down on his knees and proposed. 'Marry me, Molly,' he said."

Only Jennie is surprised, but it's because she has lived in Fairfield for only a year and doesn't know its history. She's been admitted to this group of older women because she and her husband seem to have arrived in town without friends or family support. Norma has practically adopted her.

"Jerry and I were secretly married just before Easter. I finished the school year, no one the wiser." There are nods and *um-hm*'s.

Then there is an awkward pause, partly because they all knew Jerry so well. He'd been a faithful husband and father until his death from cancer three years earlier. Claire appears to want to ask a question but holds back. Molly, her tea tray full of dishes, asks it for her.

"Most of you know, of course, that I have two grown children, neither old enough to have been the result of that pregnancy. So what happened?"

Norma rises to help carry things to the kitchen, but Molly stops her with a raised hand.

"I miscarried two weeks after our ever-so-private wedding. No one but the two families ever knew. I was out for a week with 'the flu.' That summer I started work at the A & P; Jerry enrolled at South Central Missouri in the fall; and we pretended to elope. Years later I finished high school by correspondence and took the GED. Nothing was lost, really. Nothing."

Everyone knows that much was lost, but such good friends wouldn't contradict her. Their sense of social and personal decline would be augmented by Route 66 Chapel's destruction, underscoring a regret they can't quite put a name to.

As Molly opens her mouth to speak once more, her friends can see a glistening in both eyes. But the hint of tears there is balanced by the gentle smile she offers them. The group instinctively understands that her sorrow has been muted by joy over a lifetime.

"So maybe," Molly concludes. "Maybe, I *was* just a little bit pregnant, after all."

III: First to Last

Two blocks past Norma White's Knit and Fit Shop and around the corner from the bakery, Harry Blackburn stares at the wooden last on which he repairs shoes. The form (foot-shaped, but upside-down) is mounted on a workbench before the store's front window. Harry often glances up from his stool to survey the pedestrian traffic on Eighth Street's sidewalk.

Today, however, even as he touches for perhaps the millionth time the aged and scarred mold on which he works, he is picturing more distant things. The heel he will eventually attach to one of Molly Smith's blue pumps has dropped onto his workbench as he indulges in a favorite speculation: that an original last existed long before shoes were ever invented.

Rather than assuming that an early shoe- or boot-maker invented a form on which to shape leather into the final product, Harry sees in his mind's eye some prehistoric, barefoot man stumbling through a forest. Suddenly, Early Man comes upon a mysterious shape at the base of a huge tree. Movie music, perhaps the theme from Kubrick's *2001: a Space Odyssey*, comes down from the clouds. "I could use that to shape something which covers a foot!" the original human shoemaker exclaims.

Harry doesn't say aloud the shoemaker's old joke--"the last shall be first"--but he chuckles nonetheless.

Pursuit of work (Molly's shoe) or fantasy (inventions of early humans) is, of course, serving another purpose: denial of bigger problems Harry faces. Entering his seventh decade of life, he has--suddenly and for the first time ever--fallen head-over-heels in love. Well, he guesses it's love.

Harry is woefully unpracticed in romance, and, so far at least, has suffered pangs of desire in quiet frustration. After sixty years as a single man, he believed he had perfected the life of self-denial. He lives alone in a neat apartment above the shoe shop. Its stark, functional style, checkerboard tile, and metal kitchen cabinets match his keen sense of order.

It's embarrassing, therefore, to have woken up this morning in a state of physical arousal he's not experienced for decades. In his dream, comely Ms. Thomas is sitting on his lap, her skirt pulled up. The hand that usually held the tools of his trade--at first resting on her miraculously tanned thigh--had begun to slide in a direction not expected from someone whose interest is shoes.

If town gossip has any validity, he would have been dreaming of Molly Smith, three years a widow and now solicitous of his company. Harry hopes it's her campaign to save Route 66 Chapel that's brought her into his store half a dozen times lately.

"You and your shop are such a fixture, Harry," she had said just the other day, putting a hand on his arm. After dropping off her pumps for repair, she'd asked him to step over with her to The Middleman Bakery, for "coffee and a chat."

"I *have* been in business nearly forty years," he admitted after they'd been served. He watched her spoon a bit of foam off the top of her latte. Having learned from his father to drink coffee black and whiskey straight (though he no longer does the latter), he can't get used to these exotic gourmet drinks, chock-a-block with varied ingredients.

"We need the old timers to remind people of how important such landmarks are. I worry that even more changes are being planned for our little town."

Harry feels the same way, though his manner-- squirming on the bakery's plastic faux-wicker chair--couldn't have been reassuring to Molly. Harry was uneasy because one of the forces behind change, the new town manager, was the object of his romantic dreams.

Well, "new" town manager isn't right: Marilyn Thomas is Fairfield's "first" town manager. Before, the mayor had pretty much directed growth--or its absence--in this community. Harry is google-eyed about Ms. Thomas (she insists on last names), but she has, he is quite sure, not the slightest idea of his infatuation.

"Don't we need some kind of plan for the future?" he asked Molly. Since her husband's death, she's continued the insurance agency on her own. At first, years ago, she'd just kept the books. But now she's shown herself a competent manager.

"We need to stay with our strengths, Harry. It's the shops and the small businesses--you and me, Norma, Claire--they're the heart of the community."

Harry considered reminding her that she had almost moved her store from Ninth Street to the new mall south of town when Jerry passed. It was probably only the fact that she owned the downtown building and would have had to lease in the mall that scuttled the move. He knew her business was declining like his own.

Only the rootless couple, Gene and Jennifer Grey, have tried recently to establish a new Main Street business. Scanning the empty tables around him, Harry had to think their bakery would go under soon, despite hard work and innovative promotion.

Back in his shop he picks up the heel to Molly's shoe and concentrates on gluing it in place. But thinking of Molly has brought to mind a chief ally in the Route 66 Chapel campaign, Norma White. And Norma is his second source of anxiety.

The yarn and fabric store run by Harry's longtime antagonist in local affairs is one block the other side of Main and on the opposite side of the street. Not only is Norma secretary of the local Republican Party (his counterpart, therefore), but she also seems to take the opposing side on every issue that comes up for local business. If he wants a hike in taxes and more municipal programs, she argues for cutbacks. While he is sympathetic to workers who need a higher hourly wage and more flexible work schedules, she demands that local storeowners stick together, opposing anything that smacks of a union. And, of course, she disapproves of his personal lifestyle.

"Nobody ever agrees with you," she has said for years. "Confirmed bachelors always stand alone." That has always been her way of dismissing him and his opinions. The tag of "confirmed bachelor" signifies for her a terminal state at the far end of the social continuum.

Norma acts as if Harry had deliberately ostracized himself from the human community. But he notes that he has friends and is involved in a number of organizations. The chance of a relationship with any woman, though, is complicated by a current physical problem, which makes him self-conscious about his body.

Still, he concludes, no one should be classified as an absolute outcast or, for that matter, as a social being. If he has held himself apart, Harry feels that Norma is too abrasive to form lasting relationships.

Of course, he keeps that belief to himself because he knows well how she lost Robbie Burns, the love of her life, so many years ago.

Harry admits that Norma and he do have different natures. He thinks of himself as more like that other newcomer to Fairfield, Maxwell Bridges. Max lives alone (or at least, he hasn't referred to any family), but his open, friendly manner has made him a welcome visitor at downtown shops. Harry met him when he brought in a pair of hiking boots for repair several months ago.

"New heels, I think," Mr. Bridges suggested, holding both boots upside down for Harry's inspection. He wears one of those new lightweight fabric jackets with a removable Thinsulate liner serious outdoors men prefer (and Harry doesn't) because they can fold into themselves, a pocket inverted becoming a carrying case.

"Yes, you've broken through to the hollow core there. I can do one of two things: replace the whole heel, or cut out a wedge where the wear is and insert a new one in the space."

"Soles OK?"

"Yes, they're fine. I assume you do a fair amount of walking?"

"I do now." He smiled. "But it may be a phase."

Maxwell Bridges offered no more about his past habits or plans for the future. Harry frequently sees him walking around town now, and perhaps twice a week he drops by the Heal-All. If there are no customers, Max will chat while Harry works.

They talk mostly about world affairs--the economy, the War on Terror, crises in Catholic (and other) churches. But Max is also curious about Fairfield, its history and its current condition.

Harry sees in this pleasant companion, who asks for no closer relationship, a kindred spirit. Max keeps his affairs to himself, but enjoys the company of others. Harry still isn't sure exactly where he lives, though it must be close to downtown.

Bridges has even made, it seems, a friend of Norma by knowing a lot about wool, sheep, spinning. Perhaps he'd been a farmer when he was younger. Now, he demands little of the world.

Harry has done the same all his life, lowering the bar of his expectations until he could step easily over it. He made his peace with his abilities and prospects ...until, that is, he met Marilyn Thomas.

IV: Donut Holes

"Are we going with the donuts or the donut holes tomorrow?" Jennifer asks Gene Grey the day after Molly's support group meeting. She handles the operation out front at the The Middleman Bakery while Gene runs the kitchen.

"Why can't it be some of each?"

"You're the cook. I just thought it would be less work if you concentrated on one or the other."

The couple have been in business only a year and, sadly, they've expended the capital originally put into the shop. So part of Jennifer's concern is cost. Variety of goods costs more, but more choices might bring in more customers.

Gene says, "I'm staying with what I've been doing--donuts *and* donut holes," and disappears though the swinging doors.

"Ah, these temperamental culinary artists!" whispers Jennifer sympathetically. It's clear she's fond of her coworker.

Jenny returns to moving today's last batch of honey buns from baking sheets onto display trays in the glass cabinets. Glancing up, she sees Harry Blackburn and Molly Smith turning the corner at Eighth Street. She hopes they're coming for coffee.

Their current most regular customer, Mr. Bridges, has told Jennifer and Gene they've made a good impression with managers of the surviving businesses on Main Street. The old-timers hope more young entrepreneurs will take advantage of low lease rates and general prosperity in the community. It's getting folks downtown to shop that's the big problem.

In the last decade especially, growth has come outside of town, in new residential developments and shopping centers. There's even been a modest boom filling up the industrial parks along Interstate 44 east and west of Fairfield. But the new residents design their own homes and seek out places where they can own at least an acre of land. The houses they build resemble mountain chalets and expansive beach condos.

Unlike previous generations, these Phipps County residents are not inspired to patronize small, family-run shops, which often feature the work of local craftsmen. They're satisfied buying mass-produced products with well-known brand names.

Slow business downtown and vacant real estate have contributed to the desire to raze Route 66 Chapel, though exactly what's to go in its place isn't clear. Rumors heard by the Greys include turning the site into a parking lot for university students, starting an alternative to Sixth Street for major east-west cross-town traffic, and--probably least likely--some sort of civic building (Fairfield is the county seat).

In addition to the shared problem of fewer downtown shoppers, though, the Greys face a more private challenge in their little bakery: hiding elements of personal history that would likely turn older storeowners and their patrons against them. They've disguised their motives in coming to the middle of the country. Their parents especially had wanted them to lead different lives.

"Hi, Mrs. Smith, Mr. Blackburn," Jenny says brightly, as the bell over the door announces their appearance in the store. "What can I get you today?" She raises her voice slightly, both because she assumes all older people have hearing problems and also because she and Gene pipe classical music from the local public radio station into the store all day.

Molly gives Jenny a warm smile, acknowledgment of the deeper friendship generated at last night's gathering of women. Jenny is already treated by Norma White like a daughter, and she suspects she'll have to take that role on with Mrs. Smith now as well. But it's so much easier than being the daughter she really is!

Gene, of course, plays the harder role, one they must be most careful to conceal. Jennifer is amazed they've carried that masquerade off so well the entire time they've lived in Fairfield. Their practiced roles have not raised the slightest suspicion. If they can last until spring--and if the business turns around just a little bit--all might be well in the end.

"Jenny, I'll take a honey bun, though I shouldn't," sighs Molly. "And … oh … one of your decaf lattes, grande."

"And you, Mr. Blackburn?"

"Oh, just coffee--black, please." He blows in his hands, cold from the winter air.

They move off to one of the small table-and-chair sets that fill the front of the shop. There's not room for more seating, and Jenny knows that space is a major obstacle to the store's success. They do pretty well on take-out, especially when Gene gets to prepare large orders for wedding receptions and other social gatherings. But better to have full tables all day.

The Greys love Fairfield and the neat little building they occupy. Like Mr. Blackburn at the shoe repair place around the corner, they live on their second floor. Stairs at the back of the shop take them to the middle of the apartment, which consists of a front room facing the street and an eat-in kitchen in the back. The two rooms are separated by the landing and a large bathroom with an art deco flavor--black and white tile, freestanding ivory sink and steel faucets, distinctive fixtures.

"Look at this!" Jenny had exclaimed, when she discovered the Murphy bed which pulls down from the wall. "This is living room by day, bedroom by night. It's like 'the film that's also a camera'!" She was referring to disposable cameras for the occasional (or forgetful) photographer.

"I like the privacy," Gene said, peering around one edge of the Venetian blinds to Main Street below. "And we're our own landlords, so long as we make our lease payments."

"We won't have many neighbors very close, though the university is only four blocks up on Main."

"Claire Kendrick told me students get most of what they need on campus, and do any other shopping at the malls, especially the new Full-mart. We need to find ways to bring them our direction. You're going to have to flirt with the first ones who come here."

"What about you?" Jenny laughed as if this were somehow unlikely. Gene is certainly attractive. But Jenny has always drawn the boys, at least one time unhappily.

"Most of the students are still male, you know," Gene said, acknowledging that the tough engineering curriculum and the small-town campus attract far fewer women then men. "And I don't want to look good to them!"

"You're right. We need business, but there are some limits we have to be careful about." She had sobered markedly. Then she brightened again. "How about if I be the cook upstairs since you're the baker below. We'll swap places in our partnership. Each can have different downstairs and upstairs personalities."

"What should I do up here? Sit in front room with the evening paper and smoke a pipe?"

Again, Jenny exploded in giggles. She threw her arms around Gene, and they held each other close. "We can make this work! I know we can. And it's just for another year, maybe two."

Now she carries the latte over to Mrs. Smith, who's taking delicate, small bites of her honey bun. "Thank you, dear," Molly says, lightly patting her forearm. Mr. Blackburn gives his usual unfocused smile. Jenny suspects he's being enlisted in the save Route 66 Chapel campaign the women talked about last night.

She and Gene had found that quiet retreat on one of their early walks around town a year ago. And, though not natives (or churchgoers any longer), they can see why many would want to preserve its distinctive character.

While the stone exterior links the chapel's appearance to houses and small stores in the region, the interior construction recalls European churches. Ozark Giraffe is a folk craft, using the plentiful indigenous rock as an inexpensive material for external facing. Thin slabs, each approximately one foot square but with varying shape, are embedded vertically in cement applied to the outer wood walls, creating a patchwork (giraffe-like) appearance.

The Greys were struck by the medieval, gothic look in the pews and the high pulpit set to one side. Fortunately, well placed windows on the south and east sides allow sunlight to brighten the dark wood, except, of course, on cloudy days. Still, the overall effect is of contrast, a contemporary and local exterior surrounding a conservative, foreign interior.

Mrs. Smith leans forward with new intensity as she explains something to Mr. Blackburn. Jenny takes this opportunity to step into the back, where Gene is washing the remainder of his baking pans and sheets from the day's work.

"Did you take any phone orders today?" she asks.

"I didn't tell you?" It's clear Gene is pleased. "The mayor wants us to cater town meetings now: pastries, bread, your little sandwiches. He's going to recommend us at the university."

"Steady income. That's what we need, a full schedule."

"In this case, donuts," agrees Gene with a grin. "Not holes."

V. Progress

Though she has promised to be the group's spokesperson, Molly also asked Norma and Claire to go with her to the meeting with Fairfield's mayor. Claire is a ready activist in the save Route 66 Chapel campaign. Norma, though she is less optimistic about their chances for success, wants to support her friends.

Norma's ideas of what the meeting with the mayor will be like are shaped by a favorite television show of her youth, *Gunsmoke*. She is thinking particularly of the black-and-white nature of its opening scene. (She'd viewed the show during the late 1950s, before color television came to her home in Fairfield Acres.)

Every Saturday night, *Gunsmoke* began with the same event: a showdown on the main street of Dodge City, Kansas. In the traditional gunfight of Western lore, it was good guy (sheriff Matt Dillon) versus an unnamed, but recognizably bad, outlaw. Norma loves that uncompromising view of the world, good versus evil; but she fears this time the wrong side will win.

Harry Blackburn has also been cajoled into attending, as Molly had convinced him that the future of all downtown businesses was at stake. (He also assumes Marilyn Thomas will be at the mayor's side, and he finds himself drawn to be where she is.)

"Route 66 Chapel is nothing less than our moral foundation," Molly insists at the beginning. She is following a logic she had mapped out in advance. "You can't let everything be decided on the basis of profit and loss, supply and demand."

Norma envisions Molly as a modern-day (female) hero who will save society--that is, she will preserve Route 66 Chapel. After all, the first two buildings settlers built out west were the schoolhouse and the church--well, if you don't count the saloon.

Harry thinks saving the old church is a fine idea, but his picture of the evening is framed by another erotic dream he's had about Marilyn Thomas. In this unsettling scenario she appeared as high-class customer and he as lowly shoe salesman.

Matthew Paterson listens to Molly respectfully, but does not nod in approval as do Norma and Claire. (Harry is in a bit of a fog, haunted by the events of his dream.)

A third generation Fairfield politician, Paterson had enjoyed an incumbent's status even before he was first elected mayor. Now in his fifth year of office, he is unlikely to be threatened by bluster. Matt feels he's earned the right to propose changes as well as to endorse tradition.

"Now, now Mrs. Smith, you know--har-um--perfectly well that we have more than two dozen churches within the town limits, as well as many more scattered throughout the county. We'll hardly go astray because this one unused building is--har-um--removed."

The mayor's little "har-ums" are an affectation he's inherited from his father and grandfather. It often becomes an effective distraction in meetings like this, where potential opponents end up focusing on his irritating throat clearing rather than the weaknesses of his argument.

Norma remembers that the outlaw facing the sheriff in *Gunsmoke* was always cocky, foolishly ignorant of the fact that the legendary man he faces has never been beaten. Molly must continue her attack undeterred by "har-ums."

In his dream Harry scoots one of those little shoe salesperson's stools up in front of the chair Ms. Thomas sits in. One leg crossed over the other, she is like Diddle Diddle Dumpling, one shoe off and one shoe on. Straddling the narrow stool, Harry finds his attention traveling up her long length of leg. Even in the cold, she wears short skirts.

Molly attempts a strident tone. "This particular church has historic value; it backs up on our most famous highway." The "Historic Route 66" designation has recently fortified arguments in favor of preservation along the old highway's path--or paths, as, of course, this street, Kingshighway, was superseded by the bypass around town many years ago. Still, she can claim for it a quasi-legitimate Historic Route 66 address.

Claire enters the discussion. "We'd like to know what would be done with the property if it were sold. There might be enough people--subscribers, really--who would be willing to make it a monument to our religious heritage instead of a parking lot."

Claire's family, the Johnsons, had run a department store on Main Street for nearly as long as the town has existed. She leases the building now to the university for storage. But she plans to renovate it and open an antique shop there someday.

"Ladies, I--har-um--understand your concerns. We hate to see landmarks erased. But we're talking to some developers--har-um--who may have an idea that will mean a lot to our community. Development, you know. Besides the tidy sum we'll receive in the purchase, we have to look to the future, to--har-um--development."

Harry imagines himself pulling an elegant ankle-strap sandal from the tissue of a shoe box. Scooting forward on his shoe salesman's bench, he finds his underwear bunching. As Ms. Thomas raises her foot for Harry to slip on the sandal, her short black skirt rides farther up her muscular thigh.

Molly asks the mayor, "Is this the same developer who's bought up other property downtown? Farm Industries or something?"

"It's Farmtown, Incorporated--har-um--and, yes, they feel it would fit in their long-term plans."

"But what are those long-term plans?" insists Claire. "And has town council been apprised of what they're proposing?"

Norma sucks in her breath, convinced now that what they're hearing about is already a done deal. The big bucks from out of town have moved in to take over, and there's not a thing the local people will be able to do about it. It's the same as when Full-mart moved in.

In her *Gunsmoke* scenario Norma suddenly realizes that members of the Bad Guy's outlaw gang are hidden on rooftops and around corners. It's an ambush Matt Dillon has not foreseen. Miss Kitty had better say goodbye to her sheriff/lover!

"Town Council has met with Farmtown corporate officers several times," Paterson explains. "They agree that Fairfield must change to meet--har-um--the needs of the 21st century."

Harry tries to concentrate on the question at hand, the future of the town. But, gazing at the real Ms. Thomas, and imagining his dream version of her lifting a be-sandaled foot as high as his head, he realizes he's getting excited. He doubts if his new friend, Max Bridges, would embarrass himself in this way! Nor would Max have to battle Harry's little physical problem, made more evident to him in his current position.

"I'm sorry, Mr. Mayor," Claire goes on, "You still haven't said exactly what Farmtown intends to do with the Route 66 Chapel property. As downtown business owners, I think we deserve to be consulted about what's to become of the area."

"Yes, ah, well. I'm afraid I'm not at liberty to discuss all those details, those--har-um--details at this time. But let me assure you, everyone, including people in Phipps County, will benefit--har-um--from their operation's expanding. We must go forward--har-um--or backward, you see. It's progress or--har-um--the reverse. And we want to be a part of progress."

Ms. Thomas, who up to this moment has sat quietly beside Mr. Paterson, now leans over and hands him a little slip of paper. He glances at it and then folds it in half. Norma suspects--correctly--that this is a prearranged signal to end the meeting.

"As far as I'm concerned," Norma says angrily, "the church wouldn't be much of a church anyway, even if you did save it. It would just be a building in which people had receptions, retirement parties, family celebrations."

"What's wrong with that?" Claire asks innocently.

"A church is supposed to be a church, not a dance hall, not an auditorium for political rallies, not a place to play bingo on Saturday nights. Why don't people realize that you can't mix things up, blurring the boundaries?"

"But this church is as old as Fairfield, Norma." Molly insists sadly, seeing Mr. Paterson and Ms. Thomas rise.

As he prepares to get up, Harry, one hand in his pants pocket, tries to move things around and disguise his arousal. The shoe salesman of his imagination is even less willing to stand in front of the sitting Ms. Thomas. Instead, grabbing the shoe salesman's bench with one hand behind him and the other in front, he half-scoots, half-hops it toward the door of the stockroom. He's a crazy version of a cowboy riding some quirky diminutive steed off into the sunset.

"I understand--har-um--your concerns, believe me. And I'll join you in resisting one key request from Farmtown, Inc."

"What's that?"

His announcement draws a gasp from the save-Route-66-Chapel group.

"We're not going to agree to changing the town's name. We've always been 'Fairfield.' We'll never become 'Farmtown.'"

VI: In or Out?

My daughter, Jennifer, Nelson's sister (also born by Caesarian), said she was confused when I reported the Fairfieldians' surprise at the mayor's announcement.

"It sounds to me like he's on their side," she explained. "He's going to preserve Fairfield. What's the problem?"

I realized I would have to work harder to reach the younger generation with this story. While I don't think the old and the young are hopelessly divided, sometimes an extra effort does have to be made to bridge the generation gap.

"You see," I told my Jennifer (not Jenny Grey from the bakery), "they never for a moment thought their town's name *could* change. That's what Fairfield had been for almost 150 years, since it was founded. That the idea would even come up for debate was horrifying."

"But changing the name wouldn't have been bad. Businesses remake their images all the time. It's almost an American right, to fashion yourself anew any time you find the old self doesn't suit present circumstances."

Of course, she has a point. Music groups dissolve only to reappear as new (and newly titled) bands. Politicians remake themselves with the help of public relations experts and media consultants. Brand names are ditched because of negative publicity. What would be wrong with Fairfield becoming Farmtown?

But, again, this is the story of a particular group, a 1950s generation that had seen so many changes in the previous half century that they longed for stability and order. All around them old landmarks were disappearing, and a new order was taking shape. How, they wondered, could they navigate through this constantly shifting landscape?

"Think of it this way," I offered. "Aren't there some towns that have disappeared? Think of Troy, for example. The Greeks razed it. That's really what I'm talking about.

"Ancient history, Mom! Towns don't go out of existence these days. In fact, Fairfield's still Fairfield, the place where Dad grew up."

"That's true, but only because some of the people I'm telling you about banded together to save it."

I recall Ozark novelist Don Harington's stories of a fictional mountain village in Arkansas. First settlers there were so eager for company that they told every visitor who talked of departing, "Stay more!" As Harington tells the tale, that little town (eventually known as "Stay More") is now inhabited by cockroaches, ghosts, and an occasional lost soul. The discontinuation of railroad service, the loss of agricultural markets, and prospects of milder climate and an easier lifestyle have diminished populations throughout the Midwest.

Jennifer accepts my key point, that some people probably made an effort to affect the course of events. And I continue to stress the danger they felt of takeover by outsiders, by an alien vision of their very identity.

Even the young folks in this group, the Greys, were caught up in the struggle to save Route 66 Chapel and the downtown blocks surrounding it. They recognized that, to survive and prosper, the Middleman Bakery needed a context of neighboring small shops.

This couple had fled the towns where they'd spent most of their years and chosen to hide out in a small, quiet Midwestern community. They didn't want Fairfield to draw attention to itself--and, thus, to them--by taking the radical action of changing its name. So they found themselves compelled to join in the church rescue operation, though they still hoped to work more as silent partners than as vocal activists.

If it had been up to Norma White, the Greys wouldn't have been invited to join the campaign in the first place. It was probably only her established antagonism to Harry Blackburn that led her to accept them in the group. When Harry wondered if they would be much help, Norma had to take the opposite view.

"What do they know about the way it was when we got started?" she asked at first. Molly and Claire had come back with her to the Knit and Fit Shop after the failed meeting with the mayor. They'd dragged a reluctant Harry along as well.

"I thought you liked Jenny," Claire said. "Didn't you offer to help her learn to knit?"

"Oh, she just wanted something to do when business is slow, and I told her how I've filled up my spare time for years." She waved a hand at sweaters, mittens, socks, and other knitted goods for sale on shelves along one wall of her little shop.

Harry agreed. "They've hardly been here a year. This is some kind of youthful lark, an escape. They'll be off on another scheme just when we need to take action. Children!"

"Well, now, they don't seem *that* flighty to me," Norma countered. "I mean, she's a nice girl. And I'm convinced she's been hurt by someone, someone before Gene."

"Hurt?" Molly mused. "I hadn't thought of it that way."

"They seem happy together," Claire asserted tentatively.

"You know, though ... " Molly began, then hesitated, as if embarrassed to say what she's been feeling for some time. "You know, they don't seem ... I mean, I don't feel ... that they're so terribly in love. In love."

After a pause, Claire agreed, "It is more like they're brother and sister, the best of friends."

"The state of their marriage is beside the point," Harry argued wearily. "They're different from us, outsiders and young people. They don't fit in." Mentally, he is comparing them to Max, who, though newer to town, is everyone's confidante.

"I say we bring them on board," Norma concluded, surprising everyone. But since Claire and Molly had wanted this all along, they nodded. Harry raised his eyebrows and shrugged his shoulders. Norma even volunteered to talk with them about signing a petition, which would go to town council.

Later that day, the Greys announced to Norma that they were in. However, in private the couple was still concerned about an increased public role in the Fairfield community.

"Take a look at this, too" Gene said, flipping a letter on the kitchen counter as Jenny was getting dinner together.

"We don't get mail here," Jenny asserted, despite the evidence before her. He had picked it up from their post office box, which was generally empty. "I don't see any return address, do you?"

"Check the postmark."

"Ah, I see what you mean: Johnson City." With Kingsport, Tennessee, and Bristol, Virginia, Johnson City constitutes a place known throughout the Southeast as Tri-cities. "It's got to be Taylor. You read it."

Reluctantly, Gene tore open the envelope and scanned the letter's contents. Jennifer turned back to the vegetarian lasagna she'd been preparing. Unlike the meat-and-potatoes diet of their parents' generation, their meals featured soy and dairy products, often cooked in imaginative ways.

"He's coming," Gene announced simply.

"Here?"

"Yes. He says he's taken a turn for the worse."

"Well, you know we can't say no. We're about all he's got, poor fellow."

Gene hands her the letter, which is handwritten on a single sheet. She reads it and her thoughts turn to the unhappy story of their friend Taylor.

Gene opens a beer and sits at the little dinette set. From there he can look over the rooftops of other stores. "We told him not to write unless ... "

"Except in an emergency." She begins to layer in the tomato sauce and basil, the cheeses, the pasta.

"We'll have to explain things to him, who we say we are."

"He'll cooperate. Maybe if we can help him to rest, he'll get his strength back."

"We were doing pretty well here, you know. Everybody's gotten past asking about us--where we've come from, why we chose Fairfield. And now this Chapel business has got everyone's attention, a perfect distraction."

"It's going to be hard, I know. He'll have to sleep ... well, maybe we can fit a cot on the landing."

"There's more space in the bathroom!" They both laugh at the image. It's the first light moment they've shared since they opened the letter.

They have the buoyancy of youth. Unlike Harry and the older women, who have been worn down by long battles, these two still have reserve capacity to bounce back from adversity. Their fresh start in Fairfield is testimony to their spunk, their refusal to fit into molds created by others. What they face this time, though, will be more trying than they imagine.

VII. Fire and Smoke

Then, the town's other newcomer, Mr. Bridges, saved Norma White's Knit and Fit shop from turning into a fiery inferno. Out walking early one morning, he spotted smoke rising from the buildings where the *Fairfield Mirror* had been printed for over a century. Across the street from Norma's place, the newspaper complex had been empty for several years.

The Sweet family had closed up shop five years ago, retiring *en masse* to Florida. In a deal that showed old man Sweet understood the winds of change far better than some in the younger generation, he had sold his property to a rival newspaper from several counties over. That company thought they would inherit the area's one subscriber list when they moved into the *Mirror*'s space. But their forecasts had been based on faulty assumptions.

The number of newspaper readers declined steadily as Internet readers increased, and advertisers began to prefer radio, billboard, and flyer rather than the local paper. Even new features like weekly prizes for correctly predicting professional football scores and an engaging historical serial, *Yesterday/Today*, which dramatized the founding of Fairfield, failed to boost circulation.

The paper especially believed *Yesterday/Today* would reverse slumping sales because its author was a famous Fairfield native. Willa Rogers had used the charms that won her a Miss Route 66 crown to become evening news anchor for an ABC station in St. Louis. But her written prose lacked the sex appeal of her announcer's pose--long legs crossed atop a high stool.

The *Fairfield Post* folded within two years of launching its first issue, and the building went up for sale a second time (before it nearly went up in flames). After the second paper was out of business, Norma watched the front of the building, mournfully closed up, beginning to suffer from neglect. Now its blackened exterior and boarded windows, she knew, would be an even more depressing sight.

If Max Bridges hadn't been out for an early morning constitutional, the blaze might have spread toward the old three-story hotel (also defunct) next door to the west and, given the strong wind, perhaps across the street.

In the excitement that followed--the powerful siren calling volunteer firemen, a wail of fire trucks, Main Street blocked off and traffic rerouted--most observers tended to forget who had raised the alarm in the first place. Marilyn Thomas, the town manager, however, wondered later that morning, "Wasn't that man out walking awfully early?"

She had come in at her usual time, but the mayor had been called at 5:30 a.m. by the Chief and watched the firemen at work until midmorning. With the blaze under control, he had retreated to his office.

"I don't know this Mr. Bridges--har-um. Where does he work?"

"He doesn't, at least as far as I know. He's been in town since early fall, but he has no phone listing. (I checked.) And his mailing address is a post office box."

"How old would you say he is? He might be retired."

"I find it hard to say. He's not real young, but not that old either. Somewhere in the middle, perhaps late forties."

"Well, we're lucky he's an early walker!" Paterson, who had his ancestors' heavy build, eschewed all exercise. He was sufficiently obese to be a candidate for heart trouble.

Ms. Thomas's commitment to fitness restricted the degree of esteem she felt for her boss. She understood the importance of physical appearance in their line of work. With advanced degrees in town planning and public policy, she was very ambitious. And Paterson's self indulgence encouraged her to anticipate opportunity in tiny, remote Fairfield.

Still, she was not by nature herself an early riser, and Mr. Bridges' being abroad at that hour struck her as odd. Her own schedule included a daily 90-minute visit to the Phigure Phlatterer across from the Full-mart Super Center. There she pumped iron, jogged on the tread mill, and swam half a mile. She made up for the extended lunchtime the regimen required by staying until 6:00 every evening.

It's a good thing Harry Blackburn didn't see her at the Phigure Phlatterer, where her taut body strained and stretched on a variety of machines. The bachelor's night- and daydreams would have been even more dangerous to his ascetic life if he'd seen her firm breasts and rounded buttocks snugly outlined in skintight, multicolored Speedos, her sculpted thighs and upper arms wrapped around bars and pads, the looks of fierce determination on her face aimed at perpetual refinement in form and function.

"She's smoking!" whispered Dave Jennings, the Phigure Phlatterer's principle workout specialist, when he first saw her muscles bunch and swell. Face down on a padded bench, she was hoisting weights hung from her ankles, first one, then the other. At the same time she hefted barbells to her shoulders.

"She's on fire!" corrected Rosie, his wife and the establishment's steady manager. She also felt she could see smoke coming off her husband.

As Ms. Thomas worked out on the day of the fire, she continued to wonder about the status of this Bridges guy. Retired or not, he should be paying taxes--property, automobile--or buying permits of some sort. But his name was nowhere in town records. This wasn't the main concern of her private or professional life right now, but she filed a memo in the back of her mind to see what more could be learned about him.

Others in town remarked only that Max's alert reaction to smoke had been fortuitous. The downtown merchants, who'd come to know him, thought even better of this regular customer. Norma saw the event of the fire, not Bridges' involvement, as ominous.

"Claire," she told her friend, "I'm frightened."

"Well, you should be. If that blaze had gotten any hotter, Chief Donaldson told me, they would have had a very hard time getting it under control. Did you feel the heat?"

Claire was sitting on the love seat at the back of the Knit and Fit. Norma's store was so small, that, from the door, you couldn't tell that there was a small area behind shelves and racks to sit. Norma occupied, as she usually did, a wooden office chair behind an old roll top desk.

"It's not the real smoke that worries me. You know how they say, 'Where there's smoke, there's fire.'"

"Sure."

"Claire, I'm not at all sure this fire was an accident."

"But Chief Donaldson said that those neglected cloth piles are almost surely the cause." Some discarded oily rags, used to clean the presses, had been tentatively identified as the site of combustion. "And with all that old paper lying around, there was plenty of fuel once things got started."

"Who owns that building? Is it still the Cabool people?"

"As far as I know. I think they were looking for buyers, but set the price too high initially. Somebody told me--I can't remember now who it was ... somebody told me they don't need the money. It may even be part of some tax advantage to hold onto vacant property."

"You know they own more than the building, where the presses are, and the storage area."

"Yes. The offices are separate, but just next door. And they do own quite a bit of parking space out back."

"So, except for the Short Hotel, they practically take up the rest of the block."

The Short Hotel had not been in operation for several decades. Redecorated with chrome, plastic, and other industrial materials in the 1950's, it represents one era of Fairfield history. As Norma could still remind everyone, the new chain motels, one indistinguishable from another, closed the hotel not long after the Route 66 By-pass was built. Successive owners converted the old establishment into student rooms, condominiums, and, finally, retirement apartments. Every venture had failed.

"What does that mean, though?" Claire inquired.

Norma wasn't sure it was time to reveal she had been contacted about selling her building, not once but twice.

The first time it had been a general inquiry through the mail, a chain Laundromat operation looking for downtown space. The second feeler was by phone, some representative of a firm or company who suggested others were selling around Norma and she might as well take advantage of the timing.

When she pressed the caller about whom he represented, he backed away. She even began to sense a hint of danger in his assertion that she would be especially wise to sell before this became a buyers' market. Now, with the property across the street ruined, she worried that the smoke in this case--offers to buy--might mean fire later--the threat to sell or else!

VIII. Bought and Sold

A week after the meeting with the mayor, Molly, Claire, and Norma converged on the bakery to set strategy. The goal was to inform the public that the famous Route 66 Chapel was in danger of being sold--not to a fellow towns person, but to some unknown, out-of-town conglomerate.

The older women wanted to keep Jenny up with the conversation, but she was in and out of the back waiting on other customers and helping Gene. There were two tables of college students on the other side of the room. Max Bridges had taken a chair at the table of young men, as there was nowhere else vacant.

"OK," began Molly. "I think one of the first things we need to do is find out about Farmtown, Inc.--where they're located, what other projects they've undertaken, how long they've been in operation. I can do that either on the computer or through agency contacts."

While proud of her status as an independent agent, she still had to rely on national and regional insurance companies, who underwrote the policies she sold. And they had access to directories that might provide a profile of the developers.

At one table three girls from South Central Missouri State were preparing some sort of class report. They had printed spreadsheets and pie charts, two laptops, a digital video camera.

The Middleman didn't have internet hookup. Getting wireless service was one of the items on Gene's dream list for improving the operation. His model was the suburban Starbucks.

Claire said, "I've been trying to find out exactly how much property the developers have acquired. I know a good number of lots and buildings have changed hands frequently in the last few years. There was a time when we knew who owned what around here, but so many have sold out and moved on. Why, these days … . " Her voice trailed off as if pursuing some other thought.

Norma was silent. She had not talked to her friends about what she planned to do in six months--that is, close down the Knit and Fit Store. She wondered, though, if she couldn't put it off for a time. Still, she had a retirement dream that became more attractive with each passing week.

Jenny emerged from the kitchen, holding level a tray of donuts in one hand, a second tray of donut holes in the other. She smiled at all her customers, ready, if anyone caught her eye, to bring more coffee or pastry.

"You know," Norma offered, "I think Harry Blackburn may be involved in this Farmtown operation. Did you notice he didn't really speak up at the meeting with the mayor? Maybe Farmtown's made him an offer he can't refuse."

"Oh, Harry wouldn't sell his store, Norma," said Molly, quickly. "He's really a very sweet old guy, just so … so reserved. It would be good for him to be involved in our plan."

Molly noticed Harry sneaking glances at Marilyn Thomas. The town manager was attractive, even if, Molly felt, a bit cool, too professional. Molly was embarrassed about having gained weight since her husband's death, and she'd studied Ms. Thomas's toned body jealously. She must really start exercising herself!

"What we also need," said Claire, "is a list of supporters. Maybe a petition. You and Harry could work on that together, Norma."

Norma's jaw dropped. A pained expression on Molly's face--if either Claire or Norma had noticed--would have revealed that she preferred to be the one teaming up with Harry in any such venture.

The male college students had been reading since they got their coffee. Mr. Bridges held open the St. Louis paper. When one boy took a bite of cruller, there was a flash from his silver tongue stud. Norma noticed that the other had an eyebrow bar.

It was rare to see many Miners (their school nickname) at the Middleman on weekdays. Recently, however, students had begun coming more often, the one with the tongue stud in particular. Gene feared too many of this particular crowd might drive away the few townspeople who did their shopping on Main Street.

Encouraging customers to linger and purchase, the Greys didn't close the bakery until 6:00, an hour later than other stores on Main. Since they lived right in the building and had to clean up and get ready for the next day, Gene figured they might as well be open that one extra hour. It was still not the longer hours Starbucks would offer.

When Norma didn't respond to the suggestion she work with Harry, Claire went on about another matter. "I did get Carl to see what he could find out about property owners, about transfers and such." Carl was her husband.

Molly raised her eyebrows, and Claire continued. "He says there really has been a lot of buying and selling."

Norma snorted. "That's the way with everything these days. Nobody stays put. We've become a transient society, always on the move. Americans are never in the same place two years in a row."

Claire's husband helped manage their department store for years, having come to work there as a stock boy right after the Vietnam War. He rose by effort, and by courting the owner's daughter. Their children, twin boys, were drawn from Fairfield by the siren calls of big city and big business. So Carl and Claire's generation mark the end of a respected line of local shopkeepers.

"Anyway," Claire went on, ignoring Norma, "people we've never heard of have been buying up downtown lots, but then reselling them to someone named--what is his name? Oh, Horatio Radar."

"Horatio Radar? You think he represents Farmtown, Inc.?"

"He might. As near as Carl could determine, he may now own a third of all downtown space. And, of course, the town--with its municipal buildings and parking lots--owns more than a third. We know most of the other owners."

"Goodness!" Molly exclaimed. "We're about the only people left not caught up in this scheme."

"Not *bought* up, you mean," corrected Norma.

"Bought? I guess you're right."

"Here's the way I see it: those who sold their property were seduced; and those who gained land really were paying for allegiance. It's not land being bought and sold, but people. This Radar person wants to buy the town's soul. Of course, that was bought and sold a long time ago."

She was recalling the former mayor who was so enthusiastic about the Route 66 bypass two generations ago. That event, Norma believed, began the erosion of downtown, as chain motels and fast-food restaurants quickly appeared along its path. Then there were modest shopping malls, each featuring a grocery store from one of the national chains--Krogers, A & P, Food Stuff. And finally came Full-mart, now steadily knocking off the last of the locally owned establishments.

None of these three ladies knows quite why the loss of Route 66 Chapel feels like a final blow to the community they've been so much a part of. Somehow the odd little building, even empty and neglected, represents a unifying idea for their way of life.

Norma watched Jenny burst through the swinging doors from the kitchen and come around with a rag to clean the table vacated by the coeds. She wondered if all these young people, the Greys or the students, had any idea of the past, of tradition.

She recalled customers coming up to the Knit and Fit from the Stony Court or The DC back in the good old days. Daughters, she knew, wanted to learn from her and from their mothers. They studied the yarns and talked about different stitches, wondered about plastic needles replacing wooden ones, examined the sweaters she'd knit following such difficult patterns.

Do these college girls do anything like that? Of course not! They're headed for careers, more training, the corporate ladder. Those who do marry will have spouses in different cities chasing professional success in other contexts. They'll commute alternate weekends, spending holidays with each other in vacation hideaways.

Children, if they decide to have them, will grow up in daycare, be raised by nannies from impoverished, Spanish-speaking countries, know their parents only as the exhausted couple who order out Thai food, pick up their laundry wrapped in paper or hanging in plastic, write checks for the cleaning service they assert is charging too much for doing too little.

While Norma herself stopped attending Fairfield Baptist after losing Robbie--and what came tragically after that--she still believes in the idea of church. These college girls should be preparing to teach Sunday school, to plan formal weddings, to know the comfort of funerals that process in stately fashion from Route 66 Chapel to the cemetery south of town.

If she'd lost all that herself ... tears suddenly came to her eyes. If she lost almost all that, maybe it was so she might teach someone, like Jenny, what she would have treasured if only ... if only she'd not lost Robbie and the baby.

IX. Shoes

Later that same week, Harry, at his worktable as usual, saw Norma striding down Eighth Street from Main. He hoped she was not coming here, as he doesn't feel like hearing another lecture on his incorrigible nature, "confirmed bachelor."

Claire and Molly have already bothered him again about the Rescue Route 66 Chapel Campaign (RR66CC). They've formed an official association under that name, using Claire's computer to design stationary, membership cards, and posters.

Paring life down to its essential, bread-and-butter needs, though, remains Harry's goal. Reluctantly, he acknowledges that some limited interaction with others of the species is desirable. And he might even be willing to stretch these principles for more involvement with Marilyn Thomas, however unlikely that possibility would appear to any objective observer.

Seeing Norma step through his door, Harry noted unconsciously her heel-and-toe walk. She's one of those who plant the heel of each foot firmly, then rock forward onto the toe. Most people land pretty much on the whole foot, though many pronate--roll the foot inward as the body's weight comes down in stepping.

While critical of Harry's lifestyle, Norma has always known he's good at what he does. She regularly patronizes his business. And now, of course, he's Fairfield's only shoe repair person.

The door's opening rang the little brass bell that hangs from the frame, and Norma delivered a matter of fact greeting: "Harry." He returned a similar salutation, trying to show puzzlement that she was not handing him sandals, an old handbag, something to fix.

Over the years, the Heal-All Shoe Shop has provided Harry with just the right amount and kind of human contact. He sees people every day, the great majority of whom he knows already. So they chat about family and local events when dropping off or picking up leather and canvas articles. But, the day done, Harry is alone upstairs, quite capable of amusing himself until an early bedtime. He works Saturday morning, but the rest of the weekend is his own. And a little upstairs porch in the back gives him the privacy he needs to treat his embarrassing rash.

"Do I have something for you?" Harry asked Norma, swiveling on his stool to scan the wooden shelves where brown paper bags--the kind in which kids used to pack their lunches--were arranged. (Norma decries the variety of color, shape, and design in the contemporary lunch box.) Each bag sports a cardboard tag on which is written, in neat block printing, the name of a customer, requested service, the price, and a date it is to be ready.

"No. It's about the Are-are-six-six-sea-sea petition. Claire insists we do this together."

Harry had noted from the beginning that Norma carried nothing in her hands. And he feared it would be something like this that brought her, a request to cooperate on some matter in which she would assert they share an interest. But he believes, inevitably, they will come to disagree about the project.

Heal-All's orderliness--the shelves, the bags, the tags--is a key to his modest business success. Norma (ignoring her own single status) has insisted many times that only a confirmed bachelor could maintain such a strict regimen. She knows where things are in the Knit and Fit Shop, but her system would not be apparent to anyone else.

"I guess she thinks we can use our party lists-- unofficially, of course--to canvas those who might take a stand," Harry said. "But I fear this is already a lost cause."

Norma had thought as much herself after the meeting with the mayor. Now, however, she took a different view. "It may just be that people--you know, the Martins, the Davidsons, Marlene Brentano--have been kept in the dark about it, about this Farmtown Industries group. Maybe we should try to shed some light on what's going on.

We ought to be able to work together, as many years as we've known each other."

Along the front window on the other side of the door from his workbench, Harry has a row of seats bolted together. They had been saved from the old high school auditorium when it was taken down years ago. Norma sat in one and studies the shoemaker on his stool. Snow lingered in the corners of the windowsills.

Harry wondered if, by agreeing now, he could get Norma to leave quickly. He can count on their natural antagonism to undermine the joint effort before long, anyway. As she says, they go back more than fifty years, to their earliest childhood. He knows her from experience, but also from her shoes.

Harry has learned that his customers' shoes reveal more than the nature of their walk, the heel-and-toe walkers like Norma, the over-pronaters (Molly), shufflers (Paterson). Their personality is visible in the kind of shoe they choose and the way it wears.

Young people provide him with an easy example, though they don't even come into his shop any more. Their expensive tennis shoes (illogically, not intended for tennis courts) cannot be repaired, unless, like the kids themselves, you consider duct tape appropriate material for the job. Demonstrating the disposable mentality generated by mass production and mass marketing, they throw these shoes away, often before they're worn out.

People of his and his parents' generation, like Norma, are careful with their money and their time. She has had him use a belt with a broken buckle to repair a satchel. Couldn't out-of-style hats be modernized somehow, she asked? Though she can no longer wear high heels, because of bunions, she had him disassemble her old pairs, to what purpose he could never fathom.

"Harry," Norma said, unusually contemplative, uncharacteristically confidential. "Harry, isn't it sad that the town can change, but we can't?"

"What do you mean?"

"Well, you're a confirmed bachelor, and I'm a young widow. I mean, I'm not young anymore, of course, but I've never escaped that aura, that sense of one who will lose out on the major joys of life. Family, children, a companion to grow old with. Even if I'd tried, I couldn't have changed. People wouldn't let me."

"Oh, that's not right. For one thing, it's true I've never married, never really entered into a ... never kept up with someone. But there's no reason I couldn't, even now."

Norma thought to herself, "You've had a handful of dates in your entire life," but was kind enough for once not to say it. Instead, she conceded, "I don't have as much to remember as most widows. I've no photo albums, few letters. He wasn't even alive for our first anniversary."

Harry was moved despite himself by her history and by the mournful tone in which she speaks. But he refuses to accept her logic about his own solitary state. He has friends. And now he even entertains, tentatively, some romantic aspirations, even if such hopes have an irrational basis: Marilyn Thomas's shoes.

All his life, Harry has walked on his toes. Many babies, of course, just learning to walk, don't seem to want to plant their feet flatly and firmly on surfaces. They tippy-toe around like would-be ballerinas in slippers with toe padding. Harry was one of those, his mother told him, who did so for the longest time.

One way of steadying an infant in this stage is to put shoes on him or her, those little white leather, hard-soled shoes that keep the bottoms of their feet planted on the floor. But even with those shoes (now bronzed and stored in a chest in his apartment above the Heal-All) Harry kept dancing. And, now, a lifetime of shoe repair has underscored to him how distinctive his toe-and-heel walk is among adults.

Harry is inspired to think that Marilyn Thomas's step is similar. Not that he's had a chance (yet) to study her shoes and prove this trait in patterns of wear, but seeing her stride past his storefront on Eighth Street has encouraged him to believe that they have similar natures.

And he has dreamed about the new town manager's feet, calves, thighs, and more. He believes she lands toe-first, not because of the high heels she wears but because of the way she is put together. The two of them could walk side-by-side, he thinks, stride by stride, hand-in-hand (though his rash, in such a private place, would have to be taken care of first).

"Harry," Norma interrupted his reverie. "You've always been happy as a confirmed bachelor. You never wanted anything else. But ... I don't know ... I wish, now ... I wish that things had been different. I wish they were different now."

Harry studied her. He had always assumed she chose the course she followed after Robbie's death. Fiercely independent, strong willed, hardworking businesswoman, she'd built a position and a reputation in Fairfield. Could it be that both these old-timers, thought to be fixed quantities in the local landscape, want to change who they are at this late date? And if they do, could either really step out on a new path, toe-first or heel?

X. Bodies and Spirits

The next Sunday Gene and Jenny Grey found themselves seated on one of Route 66 Chapel's dusty pews, not because they had a sudden desire to be in church, but because it was the one day they didn't work and they were seeking distraction from their current problems. In the end, though, they turned up another, even bigger problem.

They had begun with an unhurried, pleasant walk around town late in the afternoon. Soon they found themselves counting the number of businesses still operating in relation to empty buildings and lots. It was not encouraging.

"Claire has done her research," Jenny reminded Gene. "At least two thirds of the downtown space is not being used, not even for offices. Not quite a ghost town, but maybe beginning to seem like one. And I'm not sure we should really count buildings that are just for storage as full-bodied businesses."

"So, you're saying we need to get more active with the Ay-Ay-Are-Pee and the Are-are-six-six-sea-sea!" They both chuckled.

"We may have to do more than that, especially now that Taylor is coming."

They had reached the southern edge of the university campus. Turning east, they walked one block and started south down West Plains Street, continuing their informal inventory of property.

Gene gave a sigh. "You know he's going to be even thinner."

"He was practically a ghost when we left! I had hoped the new medications would help."

"If he took them the way he was supposed to!"

They followed Sixth Street back across Main to Fairfield, the third north/south street where shops, town offices, and business firms dominated. Downtown was really just these three blocks wide and five blocks long.

Missouri Street, also parallel to Main, was the next street west of Fairfield, and there the oldest, mostly stately homes of this community stood. After that was Kingshighway, or old Business Route 66. That road once had motels (Stony Court), restaurants (The DC, a diner), and gas stations (the Montgomery's Phillips 66) scattered among fine homes on large lots. A number of those old houses had recently been turned into apartments.

While Fairfield was not flat, it had still been laid out in an orderly grid. (A central town square, surrounded by city blocks, characterized Missouri towns to the west, where the land leveled out on the edge of the prairie.) Fairfield's east-west numbered streets crossed the named north-south streets from the railroad tracks up to the university.

The town outside these central blocks was irregular, with large and small blocks, loops and circles, a few winding avenues and occasional cul-de-sacs. The central figures of the RR66CC--Molly, Norma, and Claire--had all grown up in small houses on Missouri Avenue or one of its crossing streets, the town's oldest neighborhood. And, of course, they appreciated the area's symmetrical scheme, the predictable numbering, a fixed relationship among residents.

The young couple surveyed the older homes. "Would you like to live in one of those some day?" Jenny asked. Though she didn't know it, this was Mayor Paterson's expansive, three-story home. One of the town's oldest, its exterior was Ozark Giraffe.

"Not here, of course. But back home, maybe. What about you?"

"Yeah, I miss the river. I need to be on one of its wide creeks at least. And houses back there are a different style, more porch to catch the breeze in the warmer climate." She sighed at her memories.

"The trees are so different, too," Gene agreed. "Here it's all elm and oak. Well, redbud and dogwood in the spring."

"But no magnolia, no crepe myrtle, no big pines."

They had come to Kingshighway, across from the thin lot on which Route 66 Chapel stood. There was no traffic as they looked at the wooded area along the road. On the other side of those oaks was the church graveyard with modest headstones.

"We should probably put our Carolina memories away for now. They belong to a past we've sworn to bury, at least for the next few years."

"I dream about it, though, don't you? Our childhood. Everything was so good then. If only we'd known!"

"I guess I'm better at quieting those ghosts, though that might not be a good thing."

"I think of the sunsets out across the water. Remember visiting Uncle Wallace, the view he had south and west?"

A car came down Kingshighway, a family all dressed up, probably coming back from evening services. They smiled at the Greys.

"The view was wonderful," Gene said, drawn into Jenny's vision, "because you had to wind your way through the pines. The swamp was dark, and it took forever to get to the point."

"But when you finally came out into the clearing, it's so beautiful." Jenny caressed his back. "He had that great yard, the dock out into the water with the bell on a post at the end."

"Come on, let's go across." He took her hand and pulled her with him to the other side of the road.

Jenny said, "Speaking of ghosts, let's see if the chapel is haunted. Don't people say it's always unlocked?" They followed a sidewalk past the trees and the graveyard.

"It was open the first time we came here. But the mayor may have boarded it up now, prior to tearing it down!" They found the double front doors unlocked. A deepening dusk darkened the interior even more than usual.

"Did you hear something?" Jenny asked, grabbing Gene's arm. She pointed toward the front of the church.

"The doors' creaking was all I heard." He peered toward the altar, the pulpit, and the two choir pews. "But maybe there is a ghost. Ooooo-ooo!"

"Stop that. I thought … . Isn't there another door? I don't remember."

"Yeah, there's a small one on the side. Do you think someone was at the door?"

The side door led to an outside stairwell that descended along the wall of the building. At the bottom was an entrance to a single room beneath the front quarter of the sanctuary, used mainly for storage.

"I can't be sure." She shook herself. "Shoot, probably just some animal or bird. The Are-are-six-six-sea-sea needs to come over here and clean up! And look at the dust on the pews."

"This one isn't too bad." He brushed it with his hand, inspecting his fingertips. "Have a seat."

"What we probably need is a confessional." Jenny was sober.

"Oh, don't be silly."

"You're right. We have nothing to confess. It's just that I feel guilty anyway."

"Guilty?"

"Well, knowing we've become the opposite of what our parents wanted, for one thing."

"We've been over and over this," Gene said with emphasis. "We really had no choice. What matters right now is what we do here in Fairfield. We've got a business to run."

"But if the local people find out about us … "

"That we're not married, for instance!" This caused both of them to laugh nervously, as if someone were listening.

"They'd be more shocked if we were," Jenny said. After a silence, she continued. "Do you miss … ?"

"We agreed not to talk about that."

"I know, I know. Still, I was just wondering. Now and then I see someone, one of the students, who has a similar build or hairstyle."

"Well, I have noticed you eyeing tongue stud guy."

"Hmm. I do find him interesting. He's not like most of the students, all engineers. He's at the other end of the spectrum."

"He seems to be hanging out at the bakery some days. Wasn't he there until 6:00 once this week?"

This time they both hear it, a shuffling or dragging sound. It seems to come from the area of the side door, as if someone or something might be trying to enter.

"What is that?" Jenny whispered. They stood, and their breath came short. She started to brush the dust off the seat of her pants, but stopped to listen instead.

"I don't know, but I believe it's time to get out of here."

They went quietly out the double doors, holding hands and scanning the darkness around them. Back on well-lighted Kingshighway, a block from the church, they breathed more easily. But they both knew they couldn't leave all their worries behind so easily. They'd already tried it once and failed.

Volume Two. Gender
Chapter I. Topsy-turvy

To the old-timers of Fairfield, Claire and Carl Kendrick represented the ideal married couple. Well, they did until the RR66CC came along. Then, like so many other things around town, their perfectly balanced union began to show cracks of division and contradiction.

One day in the early stages of the campaign, Claire's best friend, Molly Smith, asked her if Carl was feeling all right. Molly said, "He seems to me--I don't know--distracted, I guess."

"Carl's fine. He likes his retirement." At the time, Molly didn't note that "retirement" was attached to Carl ("his"), not to Claire also (which would have been "our").

Claire had come by the office to see if Molly's agency connections had turned up additional information about Farmtown Industries, Inc. They were sitting in the reception area.

"I know he's been playing golf more," agreed Molly. "And you have your summer house."

Everyone knew the story of the Kendricks' falling in love at first sight, almost as children, when he came to work in her daddy's store. Then, he went off to war. (That "mess in Vietnam," they said. Still, they gave him credit for serving his country in the time-honored role of supply sergeant.) Home, he picked up with family and work right where he'd left off, not the least bit affected by his experience. Or so it seemed.

The couple raised two children, which was deemed statistically appropriate for a couple of the babyboomer generation. And then, after thirty-some years running a family business (at a fairly early point Carl had taken over from Claire's father), they closed the department store, built a vacation cottage at Lake of the Ozarks, and began to attend Elder Hostels in interesting locations.

Through all of that, they had never been known to argue in public; they continued the lovers' habit of touching each other frequently; and one finished the spouse's sentence without either seeming to notice.

As they grew older, the couple even tended to look more and more alike--middle-aged spread rounding them into similar shapes, though Carl was larger in nearly all categories. "We're salt and pepper shakers," joked Carl. "A set." Claire would show her satisfaction in a broad smile.

"I think Carl wishes we'd spend more time at our cottage," Claire admitted to Molly, inspecting the packet of documents she had handed her. "Except for golf, he has trouble filling up his days. And he can get in the way around the house."

Then Claire added as an afterthought. "Of course, I'm not complaining about that sweet man, Lord knows." She had realized that Molly, a widow after 35 years of marriage, had no Jerry to worry about.

"Well, I was just wondering ... " Molly trailed off. For her part, she didn't want to say that Carl had talked to her recently. He said he wasn't happy with Claire's involvement in RR66CC. And he'd seemed so down, Molly thought.

She tried to speak to Harry about it, but that old rascal was dense as ever about other people's problems. All he had noticed was that Carl sometimes accompanied Max Bridges on strolls about town, talking intently as they walked.

"Anyway, I'm concerned about all of us, not just Carl. You see what my friend Dan Robinson says? Right there." She turned the pages in Claire's hands until they were at the last one.

"I see. The money trail disappears into these mysterious corporations whose only addresses are overseas post office boxes."

"And they have short histories. They come, they go, whoever it is that's buying up Fairfield."

Claire chuckled. "That's what Norma says about everyone these days. No roots, no history, no long-term commitments. The world's gone topsy-turvy according to her."

Molly joined her in laughter. But her own experience after Jerry's sickness and death matched Norma's sense of things gone haywire. She was still struggling to keep her bearings.

Claire's so lucky to have Carl, thought Molly. She was not at all sure Claire appreciated that fact, even if he'd been acting more out of it than he used to. At least he was a companion. He balanced Claire and gave her stability, an anchor through time.

Molly knew her own love story was a fine one. The Route 66 Chapel proposal--although only recently confessed to her friends--is as romantic as something from a movie.

Sure, they'd had some troubles along the way, like that flirtation she carried on with Tom Simmons when the two couples used to share a baby-sitter and go out dancing together. And Jerry's lack of attention during the early years of building their insurance business had grated. There were also arguments over what careers their children should pursue after college.

But they'd always gotten past the hard places, always together. You can't be together with a ghost, Molly told herself, can you? She felt like half a person these days, still surprised at the smooth covers on the other half of her bed, the lack of daily observations offered over the top of the morning paper, no one to usher her into their pew at church.

If she were Carl's wife, she'd be paying more attention to his moods. She wouldn't let him mope or wander the streets with a virtual stranger. She'd make sure no topsy-turvy turn of events broke them apart!

"Just what I feared," Claire exclaimed, throwing the packet of papers down on the coffee table in front of them. "We're up against international conglomerates, big money!"

"The thing that gets me," Molly said, "is what are they planning to do with all this property? Even if they filled up all the buildings with shops, they'd have a hard time competing against Full-mart. People have gotten accustomed to malls, and you can't transform a whole downtown into a mall. Can you?"

"The mayor's certainly not going to tell us their plan. He's been 'bought and sold,' as Norma says. We need to figure out a way to make them show their hand, so we know what we're fighting, who the opposition is."

Claire sighed. "I'm not sure the RR66CC is a genuine opponent at this point. It's looking too much like David and Goliath so far."

"What about our hosting a public event, a consciousness raiser of some sort?"

Claire brightened. "Not just saving Route 66 Chapel, but learning the fate of Fairfield? Yes, that's good. What could it be? And where would we have it?"

They both puzzled over these questions. Then Molly said, "How about at the Middleman Bakery?"

"Not very big, though."

"Oooh, you're right. Still, we could have them cater it."

"You're just like Norma, wanting to adopt that young couple!"

When Claire said this, Molly thought how much the Greys reminded her of herself and Jerry when they were young. Maybe they're like Carl and Claire as well, another perfect couple.

The problem with perfect couples is that they're not forever. Like a good many in her generation, Molly had survived the traditional early pitfalls only to find there was more work to be done to keep an older relationship healthy. He blamed her for his diminishing libido, an almost inevitable aspect of aging. And she was unwilling to consider some of the remedies he had read about in questionable advice columns. Many long-standing unions have crumbled under such pressures.

But the saddest, Molly thinks--well aware that she's feeling sorry for herself--is her own situation: outliving the one you've loved too long to think seriously about marrying someone else. Must she spend the rest of her life alone? What a silly thing to be, a widow!

"Now I have to tell you what I've found out," Claire said.

"What? About Farmtown?"

"That's right. Carl has an old Army buddy in New York who's in the investment business. And he's asked around." Claire pauses. "It isn't good, Molly."

"Tell me."

"Apparently they bought up another whole downtown. In one of the Dakotas, I can't remember which. (I can never keep them straight!) Anyway, the town was about the same size as Fairfield."

"What did they do when they'd owned all the property? Put in their own companies? Add residential development? Raze it all for some huge convention center?"

Claire hesitates. "Now, if Patrick has it right … . Well, he says they … they did tear down all the buildings … and then broke up the pavement … plowed the ground and … planted wheat!"

II. Dividing Lines

Although neither Claire nor Molly had spoken of it, each thought about recruiting Max Bridges as a potential male ally in the RR66CC campaign. True, they didn't know exactly where he lived--or how he lived, for that matter--but he seemed to be a downtown resident. And everyone agreed that he was interested in town politics, the issues that faced the community.

Unlike the Greys, he had no accent (or at least none that Molly or Claire recognized). While he was certainly older than Gene and Jenny, he was comfortable in their (and students') company. But he was also found congenial by Fairfield seniors.

He was seen regularly in Harry's shop--having guy talk. And now he went out walking with Carl. But women liked him as well and were sometimes surprised by his expression of traditionally feminine interests.

At the Knit and Fit Shop Max recognized rare yarn, knew the relationship between size of needles and kind of pattern, talked of styles associated with different nationalities. Norma said she wouldn't be surprised to find that he'd been in the business at one point, perhaps a supplier or distributor.

Where did he come from, north or south of the Mason-Dixon Line? For that matter, had he grown up east or west of the nation's other dividing line, the Mississippi River? As he talked about current events, he seemed to suggest he had traveled widely, knew the country's many regions, and had seen the standard landmarks without residing near one only.

Claire had once heard him explaining the legend of Route 66 to a table of students at the Middleman, including the one Gene called "tongue-stud guy." Not only did Max know the history of the Mother Road, but he'd talked about roadside attractions as if he'd driven the 2,600-mile length of the highway and seen them all. He had spoken nostalgically of staying at the Coral Court in St. Louis and at Fairfield's Banner Hotel, both now, sadly, gone.

Molly had originally conceived of this wanderer with a sense of history as a possible new officer of the RR66CC during a visit to the shoe shop. Max had been in an extended discussion with Harry, and she'd found herself drawn to their topic.

"I did the obligatory tour of Historic Colonyville a few years back," Max had been saying just as Molly swung the door open. "Ever been there?"

Turning, Harry had said to her, "Oh, hi, Molly." Then back to Max, "No. Excuse me a minute." Again to Molly, "Yes?"

"Hello, Max. Nice to see you. Harry, I'm not here on shoe business exactly. More just visiting.

Please go on and finish what you were saying. I can wait."

Sitting in one of the old auditorium seats, she hadn't thought this conversation would go very far. Asking Harry if he'd been to Colonyville would have been a rhetorical question from anyone, like Molly, who knew him. Harry counted his visits outside of Phipps County on one hand.

Twenty years ago he'd been to the funeral of the shoe repairman who had owned Heal-All before him and finally retired to live up near his daughter in St. Louis. Alex Manette had trained Harry, just graduated from high school, as an apprentice. And not long after completing his apprenticeship, Harry traveled to Kansas City for a long weekend. But not even his closest friends knew the purpose of that trip.

"No," Harry had admitted. "But I have read about Colonyville and Jamestown, sites I suppose all Americans *should* visit."

"That's right," Molly had agreed, joining the conversation from her seat. "Jerry and I took the girls when they were teenagers. It taught them about our nation's founding."

"It does have a lot to offer," Max had said. "Especially, for me, it demonstrates how hard life was for settlers coming from the Old World to the New."

"I guess everything is different, there and here," Harry had added. "A fallen Old World versus the Puritans' New Eden."

"Certainly the climate was different, as the Virginia location is farther south than anything in England."

"They were determined to break free of England," Molly had pointed out.

"One thing bothered me at Colonyville, though," Max had gone on. "There were two kinds of passes: the day ticket and the extended pass, good for several days."

"Why is that a problem? Sounds basically like a standard markdown for volume."

"It's not the principle of discounting; it's the labels they attach. If you enroll for the year, your pass reads 'True Patriot.' If you are only coming for the day, you're ... 'Visitor,' I think it is. It's as if they want to divide us into loyal Americans and Americans whose allegiance is questionable."

Harry had shaken his head. "You don't wear the pass, though, do you? Isn't it just a ticket you can slip in your pocket."

"Oh, no. It's a badge that must be visible at all times."

Molly had sat up straight and huffed, "Well, I don't see anything wrong with that. In my opinion, we don't have enough 'true patriots' these days."

Max had been gentle in his response, but there had been strong feeling in his words. "Perhaps, but I'm not sure patriotism is measured by how much money you have to spend on vacation."

"I'd have to go as a 'Visitor,'" Harry had volunteered.

"At one time in my life," Max had admitted, "they'd have had to invent a new category for me, someone who can only look in from the outside. Perhaps they'll call that the 'Traitor.'"

"You're being too critical." Molly had shifted in her seat, discomfited by statements that to her were vaguely disloyal. "You know, we have a Patriot Act now. Maybe that's a better way to measure who's serving the country." She really knew nothing about the particulars of that legislation.

Max's eyebrows had risen. "Pardon me for saying it, but the 'Patriot' Act assumes that we're all probably 'Traitors.' It lets the government review your bank transactions, your phone records, even what books you check out of a public library."

"Public libraries?" Harry had questioned. "Isn't that something Ben Franklin insisted on as central to a democracy?"

All of a sudden, Molly had felt outnumbered by adversaries who refused to accept that there are good guys and bad guys in this world. She had risen (again stiffly), wished the two friends a good day, and gone out the door, less willing than when she'd come in to think of Max Bridges' help as necessary to saving Route 66 Chapel.

Still, when she learned that day in Claire's office that her home town might be turned into an agricultural factory, she realized they probably needed every bit of help they could get. "With all the other land in that region," she said to Claire, "why plow up a city?"

"I know it sounds bizarre," Claire responded, "a reverse of what one of those ancient armies did-- which was it?--sowing salt where a city once stood. But that's what Carl said he was told."

"We need to check this rumor out. If it's true, maybe we do have a way to combat Farmtown, Inc. Fairfield plowed under! No one's going to accept that any more than that Hillbillyville idea some out-of-towners tried to promote some thirty years ago."

Claire picked up the papers again and weighed them in her hand. "One thing we must have is more men publicly on our side. The mayor and his cohorts can ignore a bunch of women."

"You're right. We'll be dismissed as silly housewives who know nothing about the real world--about *'progress, har-um.'*"

"Carl is with us in sentiment, of course, but he doesn't want to take on any specific tasks. And we have Gene, at the bakery. I think maybe one of us should ask if he'll accept a leadership role, perhaps 'board member,' which sounds important but doesn't necessarily mean much work."

"You do that, and I'll speak with Harry again. He's got to realize his entire way of life is in danger."

Claire rose, handing the packet of papers back to Molly with a sigh. "The Greys are such a cute couple, aren't they! They're trying so hard, and they're completely on their own. I don't even know where they're from, do you? Where their family is?"

Molly stood, more slowly and stiffly than she'd like. "Norma has figured out they're from the South somewhere, but their accents told us that on the first day they were in town."

"Well, we don't hold being Southerners against them," said Claire moving toward the door. "Missouri's famous for compromise, as we all know--a border state. Everyone can find a place."

Molly, holding the door open as Claire stepped onto the sidewalk, concluded, "They can find a place right now, while there's still a town left to fit into. But what are we going to be when we're Farmtown, U.S.A., a field of yellow corn?"

III. Fairfield Prime

The concept of the RR66CC event took greater shape in Claire's mind as she walked from Molly's office. It would be a rally, she concluded, for all of Fairfield, and not just about saving Route 66 Chapel. Yes, a civic celebration and an important announcement ... but of what? A new initiative. That was it.

It would be an initiative to ... ? Okay, how about to remember the 1950s, a great time in American history? And we could feature the distinctive style of Fairfield's downtown buildings and furnishings. This might even draw in people connected with the university and local industry.

Claire reached the bakery at a propitious moment in her creative imaginings. Jenny was seated at one one of the tables with Norma, looking at catalogs for store furnishings. So it was an opportune time to make the pitch to Gene, who was having a cup of mocha on his break.

(At least he wasn't drinking Coca Cola, Claire told herself, like so many of the young people. She'd read recently that soft drinks had replaced coffee as the nation's first drink of the day. More evidence of the general downward trend of civilization! How could people accomplish anything if they didn't begin the day with a cup of coffee!)

"Don't get me anything," she waved to Jenny. "I'm here on business." She sat at his table, explaining, "Gene is the one I need to talk to."

He raised his eyebrows and cleared his throat. "What can I do for you, Mrs. Kendrick?"

"Well, for one thing, it involves catering."

The other two went back to examining possibilities for modernizing the bakery's interior. Jenny had asked Norma's advice about redecorating, thinking perhaps the Middleman's look was a bit dated for the more trendy coffees and pastries they offered. But she wanted to be careful not to turn away any older customers.

Claire told Gene, "We're moving forward in our campaign to save the Chapel. There's going to be a town meeting, sort of, to drum up support. And we were hoping you could cater the event."

"We'd be more than happy to, Mrs. Kendrick. Inside the Chapel? It's too cold to do anything outside this time of year."

"We'll have to check out the furnace, of course. Refreshments will draw the crowd. We can have speakers, or consciousness raisers, really. Technically, the building is not now a church."

"It's probably never going to be a church again," Norma said over her shoulder.

"Norma, that's not the issue right now."

Gene said to Claire, "Rally the troops, yes, I understand. You'll want finger food then, and hot and cold drinks."

Claire let Gene go over the possibilities, holding off on the second goal of her visit: recruiting him as a new officer in the RR66CC. At the same time, her mind was continuing to assemble the parts of her rally to celebrate the town and Fairfield Prime, a local derivative of art deco.

Nationally and internationally, art deco had its origins in a celebration of Modernism, of American and European progress in the 1920s. Its streamlined look and geometric patterns were related to abstract art, but Fairfield's use of the style at a later time was more an endorsement of the principles of scientific progress and national achievement.

Postwar America was flexing its new military might in the first decade of the Cold War. The arsenal that had defeated Japan and Germany was now needed as a deterrent to Soviet aggression. Against the dark, global forces of Fascism and Communism, remote and tiny Fairfield felt it was adding its little bit to the principle of light.

The community was home to a number of veterans, many still connected to nearby Fort Leonard Wood. All were committed to the West's battle with the monolith behind the Iron Curtain. And the community's appreciation of military and industrial prowess was augmented by the local college's emphasis on engineering and the success of emerging small industries outside of town.

As a result, many of the downtown buildings (including where the Middleman was housed), featured black and white tile floors. Their one-piece, sculpted, stand-alone porcelain sinks were stark shapes set off by mono color walls. Many buildings on the university campus and some homes built close to downtown had chrome or steel doorknobs, faucets, and fixtures.

Everything in Fairfield Prime was clean and polished, boundaries were precise, surfaces were solid. A man's white shirt against the slick fabric of a dark business suit, as well as the sharp click of a woman's high heels on a sparkling hotel lobby floor, marked the crisp efficiency and sense of purpose town leaders felt at the time were its driving forces.

"I think," Claire said, "we should have a short program--less than an hour--to remind everyone about Fairfield Prime, then uncover the food. Let people meet and chat with the speakers."

"What kind of numbers are you thinking about?"

"That depends on who we can get to appear. Say, here's an idea: you might want to talk about how you and Jenny, outsiders, were won over by old Fairfield's charm. I bet you're accomplished public speakers."

"Well ... ."

"Think about how it would advertise your business. Your personal qualities. People would connect your good looks and broad smile with the Middleman."

Norma, who had been listening to the end of this conversation, said to Gene, "With Jenny there, you'd be a hit, the perfect couple."

The young couple exchanged a glance.

"You don't have to say 'yes' today," Claire conceded diplomatically. "Just think about it, how it might help the Middleman ... and, of course, Fairfield. And it would surely lead to other things," she concluded vaguely.

Jenny asked, "What was that you said would be discussed? 'Fairfield Prime?'"

Norma turned around in her chair to explain its history. Her shop had the characteristic black and white tile floor too, though it had such small squares and she stocked so much material, you might not notice it unless you were alerted beforehand.

Fairfield Prime, she said, was inspired by things that could not be divided--prime colors, prime numbers, prime movers--but which, in combination, order the universe. Basic colors create the rainbow; numbers that are products only of themselves and one can count infinity; the hand of God in a Renaissance universe put the stars in motion, which in turn moved everything else.

Claire added something a faculty member who went to her church once told her. There's another kind of prime mover, she said, but she couldn't explain the idea fully.

When engineers say 'prime mover, he had told her, they're talking about whatever drives a generator. The more mechanical energy applied, the more electrical energy produced, apparently. She took this to mean vaguely that it's a kind of elemental force. And that's what she wanted to apply to the Fairfield Prime Rally, powerful force.

"So, Mr. and Mrs. Grey," concluded Claire, "you are formally invited to be a part of this new initiative. Let us know when you decide whether or not you accept the invitation."

Rising, she shook Gene's hand, waved goodbye to Jenny and Norma, and went toward the door. She'd return later, she decided, to the idea of Gene as RR66CC ombudsman.

Underneath her enthusiasm, though, Claire was feeling a bit guilty. One of the town's best examples of Fairfield Prime was the Johnson building, right now leased for storage to the university. You couldn't even see the characteristic tile floor, covered by file cabinets, old classroom furniture, miscellaneous out-of-date equipment. Some fine old steel shelving and cases had been sold for scrap. And common fluorescent bulbs had replaced glass globe lights in the 1960's.

Even if Claire followed through on her plan to use the building as an antique store, it would be hard to refurbish it in the manner of its glory days. And Carl, only vaguely interested in that or any project, would surely oppose expensive renovation.

Back in the store, Norma asked Jenny, "Do you have good insurance?"

"Insurance? A small policy. Is there a reason you ask?"

"Oh, just thinking about all this costing a bit more." Norma pointed to the catalogs, though Jenny saw a more worried look on the older woman's face. "You want to be protected, in case of … accident."

She paused, then added, "There's been a fire downtown, you know. A fire that nearly burned a city block."

IV. Flavor

The call came a week before the RR66CC's planned rally.

"Where is he?" Jenny asked, knowing by Gene's tone and manner that it was their friend Taylor.

"He's at the old bakery, down from the bus station. We'd better drive to get him."

The former Greatbuns Bread Company building was only a few blocks from the Middleman, so Jenny understood this to mean that Taylor wasn't strong enough to walk. She gave a shiver at the prospect of going out (it was 10:00 o'clock at night) and at what this would mean for their life in Fairfield.

There was irony in Taylor's coming here, as he had been the one who first told the Greys it would be a nice place to relocate. While he'd never lived here himself, apparently he had relatives who described it as a peaceful little town nestled in the Ozark foothills. It sounded like just the place for their retreat.

Pulling up in front of the bus station (the same beige brick building that used to be a major stop along Route 66), Gene and Jenny saw their friend huddled in the entryway. Even though they expected the worst, his gaunt features shocked them. "He's dying," each thought.

People sick with AIDS had treatment available at this time, of course, but they had to take the drugs religiously. And if other drugs were still in the patient's life, the decline could be rapid. For reasons he never fully explained, whatever was in Taylor's past drove him to relapses rather than remission.

Gene helped him into the front, as it was easier to lower himself onto that seat. Jenny took over driving.

"You haven't eaten, have you?" she asked.

"Not for a ... well, for a few days probably."

"We'll warm up some soup," Gene said, patting his shoulder. Then, to change the subject, he asked, "Do you know anything about what you're seeing along here? I know you're familiar with Fairfield's history."

"Ha, I do know about that place." He waved at the Greatbuns sign, faded and chipped. "Like Missouri Pure Milk, or so I was told, it was a major supplier for the whole county, run by a Phipps County family. The local Wonder Bread, but gone with progress, it looks to me." Beneath their logos was printed "Prime White Bread."

Greatbuns Bakery had dominated the area market until the supermarket chains prohibited stocking of any but their own brands. The business held on for a few years, selling in their own shops and in the last independent grocery store on Main Street. Now the two-story brick building stood vacant.

A similar end had come to Missouri Pure Milk. At the close of the war, they were delivering bottles to the doorsteps of a majority of Fairfield's homes. Local restaurants served MPM, along with Greatbuns bread. But they, too, were steadily undermined by the lower prices big dairy farms in other states offered to regional and national supermarkets.

Greatbuns had prospered by featuring buns before McDonalds arrived, but the yellow arches made home cooked burgers less appetizing. While they also baked loaf bread, their billboard and newspaper ads always pictured a top bun hovering above the inverted bottom bun, like some flying saucer. Between the two thin domes were the elongated letters "G-R-E-A-T."

"Is there a shoe repair place in town?" Taylor asked softly. Jenny felt it was tasking all his reserve energy to speak.

"Yes, do you need some work done?" She had noted that his running shoes were coming apart, but Harry couldn't repair that material.

"Oh, no. Just remembering what I heard, sort of famous places in Fairfield. Greatbuns, shoe repair, the college, and ... um, some kind of fabric store."

"Norma White's Knit and Fit Shop, probably. She's a friend, just around the corner from us. But," she brightened, "the Middleman Bakery is clearly the store of the future!"

Taylor had to rest halfway up the stairs. Jenny stayed with him, and Gene went ahead to warm the Pasta E Fagioli. They'd made it for dinner the night before and frozen two extra containers.

The Greys had put a metal cot on the landing, the only extra space there was in their cramped quarters. Taylor sat down on the blankets, slumping back against the wall. At least he wouldn't have to make much effort to reach the bathroom. But Jenny's heart pained as she watched him slide a gym bag (all he had with him) underneath the cot.

He was pitiful, but she also felt a lesser sorrow for herself and Gene, whose private lives had been, in a sense, invaded. Even at her relatively young age, she'd learned that the difference between sick or well often determines a state of happiness or sorrow. Now sickness was at the heart of their home.

Still, she announced with satisfaction, "There. This is your little corner of our world. The bathroom right here, the kitchen to the left. The living room, which doubles as our bedroom, is the other way."

Jenny stepped into the kitchen, though she feared Taylor might fall asleep before she came back. She wanted to talk with Gene and see if they agreed on what was to be done.

Her memory of Taylor as she had first seen him was in sharp contrast to the emaciated figure resting on the cot. She had met him at an ice cream parlor frequented by college kids.

Taylor had been engaged with the store's manager in a spirited debate about ice cream. Mr. Phillips (of Phillips' 66 Flavors) was proud of his many homemade specialties.

"But good old plain vanilla is always the base, don't you see," Taylor said, waving a hand at the double rows of tubs that contained Pitiless Peach Supreme, Butterscotch Itch, Hint of Peppermint, and many more. The manager was scooping from the vanilla.

"In this world," Taylor went on as if he were more advanced than his eighteen years, "you've got your basics: chocolate and vanilla. And that's good, see. They're the poles, the ends of the continuum, the frame of reference. Everything else is just a mixture of this and that. Give me the elemental, the core, one or the other."

Jenny, standing in line, giggled at his declaration.

Taylor turned to her immediately and asked, "Am I right?"

She smiled and pointed to the manager, who was holding out Taylor's cone with its single scoop of ice cream.

Taylor took the cone, handed Mr. Phillips his money, and turned back to Jenny. "You've got to have your chocolate and vanilla. Take away any of the others ... " Another sweep of his hand behind him. "Take away any of the others and you still have ice cream as we've always known it. But take those two away, you've got ... you've got ... chaos!"

Jenny laughed again, but admitted, "Well, I sort of see your point." Looking over his shoulder at the manager, though, she said, "Still, really, what I want is a double-dip cone--Dapple Apple and Graham Cracker Crusty."

"Oooh, rebuffed again," Taylor grimaced. "But, if you'll let me join you while you eat your cone, I bet I can win you over."

Even though Trinity was a small (no longer church-related) private college, they had not met on campus. He was a freshman, she a senior, so they moved in different spheres. But she accepted his invitation. It didn't take her long to guess that his exuberant public manner was hiding a vulnerable private side.

The more they talked (a good while after their ice creams were gone), the more she felt he was a boy in trouble. Was he already succumbing to the temptations of being away from parents, drinking or experimenting with drugs? Had he, coming from a protected home environment, been overwhelmed with choices or by academic challenges? Was he confused about his sexuality in an age when old stereotypes were being exploded?

Jenny couldn't tell. But she felt enough sympathy for him to give him her phone number and agree she'd have ice cream again with him sometime (so long as her choices were not limited to chocolate and vanilla). She made it clear that she was romantically involved elsewhere.

When she and Gene decided to disappear from that life, she worried most about what would happen to Vanilla Boy. The trajectory of his life from their first ice cream social was a steady, downward spiral. In the last weeks they were there, he was cutting classes, out of touch for days at a time, wild-eyed and confused when she did see him.

She was sure he would flunk out, but he said he'd never go back to live with his stepparents (he confessed to her that both of his biological parents were dead). Looking now at the exhausted man on the landing, Jenny believed he had not just dropped out of college, but out of life itself.

V. The Tubes

"The mayor has vetoed the rally!" Molly told Claire. "He says we have no permit and that he can't grant one."

"He's opposed to celebrating Fairfield, our history and achievements?" asked the astonished Claire, who had been studying a blueprint spread out on a desktop. She straightened up to face Molly and Norma. "That's not going to sit well with voters."

Molly shrugged. "I don't know. He's got a flimsy excuse, probably cooked up by that Ms. Thomas, the mysterious town manager." She looked around the old Johnson department Store. "Carl said on the phone we'd find you here. What are you doing?"

An area on one side of the front doors had been cleared of the university's material. The desk on which the blueprints lay was centered on a platform, perhaps a foot high and 150 feet square. There was where the old office had been, though the walls around it had been taken out.

"You know I've always meant to make the building into an antique store. It's time I got past the planning stage." She gestured toward the blueprint. "And on with implementation."

It was a good building for an antique store, old enough itself to represent an earlier era. The last major renovation, done in Fairfield Prime, had been finished in 1958.

The characteristic black and white tile floor was remarkably well preserved with few chips or marks. Though somewhat faded, the ebony walls were clean, and black wood trim neatly framed the front windows and double doors. But the most distinctive feature of the building was the pneumatic tube delivery system installed before World War II that unified the entire operation.

Rather than use cash registers at Johnson's Store, each sales clerk totaled the bill on a hand-crank adding machine, put the resulting paper slip and the customer's money or check into a carrier, and shot the cylinder off to a central desk in the office. First Claire's father, then Carl, later a series of his managers received tickets and money from the store's separate stations--men's clothing, women's clothing, children's, etc. They returned the carriers with change and receipts.

Claire's father, who installed the system, referred to it as his "octopus," or sometimes as the "Big O," because it's four stations required eight tubes. Joking, he claimed his "arms" could catch any employee who wasn't sharp about his or her work.

A soft hum was generated by the system's blower, and, when clerks pulled opened a cover to insert a carrier at one of the tube stops, customers could hear air being drawn inward. The covers had rubber seals and the carriers' ends had rubber stops, so they made no sound leaving and only a soft bump on arrival.

Air was drawn into a central basement unit, generating suction, and then traveled a complete circuit back to the starting point. Carriers were stopped when they fell in a short exit tube at a station, but air continued its global circulation.

Molly explained to Claire what she and Norma had learned. "He says we can't have a public rally in the Chapel because it violates the separation between church and state."

Claire protested, "But when we wanted to save the Chapel, he said it was no longer functioning, not a church anymore."

"It's his version of Catch-22. If we claim the Chapel needs to be saved, it's a church and we can't have a meeting there. If we say there's no need for a rally, that means the building is just a building, so we could meet there if we wanted to."

Norma nodded, rolling her eyes to the ceiling. "That's circular reasoning if I've ever heard it. But, surprise, surprise--what did we think we'd hear from a politician?"

The Big O's chrome tubes, which were attached to upright posts and hung from the ceiling by silver rods, reflected the light from Claire's desk. Their paths looped over and under each other on their way to and from the office. The carriers were also chrome with a dark felt interior, so even the coins rode noiselessly back and forth. The whole network resembled a complex rail system in a heavily populated urban district.

Norma has always been an especially enthusiastic fan of the Johnson Store's pneumatic delivery system because the tubes are all one-way: up to the office, or back to a service center. Each stop is clearly labeled, and discrete arrows indicate the direction of travel on every tube. For her, it was the way Route 66 had operated in its heyday, before the reversible third lane signaled an end to order, confusions of up and down, left and right, this way or that.

Molly insisted, "We've got to come up with a plan. I think the fact that he's tried to block us means he's worried we might actually be successful."

Claire mused. "I'm sure that Town Manager has a lot to do with this. You know where I saw her last week?"

"No."

"In Harry's shop. I think she's trying to get him over to the mayor's side. I bet she's connected to Farmtown, Inc. somehow. And I worry about him."

Molly said, "I've been talking to Harry all along. Surely he understands he can't give up his work. What would he do? He lives above the shop, too, so that's home to him."

Claire said, "I don't know. He may be a bit … um … smitten with Ms. Thomas."

"Smitten?" snorted Norma. "He's never been smitten in his life. And he's too old now for any romantic nonsense."

Molly asked Claire, "Tell us what you saw."

"Well, I was just walking past. You know you can see him at his work table in the window. And you could sure see her because she was wearing one of those skintight exercise outfits, every color in the rainbow on it in stripes and swooshes and whatnot."

"Hmp," said Norma. While knitwear could have patterns, she thought it should be consistent throughout the article. The patches and logos (and holes!) young people applied to clothes were all wrong.

"I assumed she was just there for some repair work. But then she turned around, put her back to him, and pointed at, I guess, the zipper on her pants, up near the top."

"Oh-oh," said Molly, clicking her tongue in the back of her throat. "I bet that zipper went right down the middle."

"That's exactly right. If you ask me, she was showing him her … her derriere. Those pants were so tight you could see things jiggle."

"I hate seeing an old man with a young woman," said Norma. "He grizzled and gray, and she all firm but bouncy."

Molly sighed. She knew the difference between Ms. Thomas' bouncy behind and her own aging bottom. "And it doesn't happen the other way around, does it? When we lose our men, some younger replacement isn't knocking at the door."

Claire went on. "Then she turned around and pointed to the zipper in the front at the top."

"Of course! Probably open halfway down."

Norma exploded with something approaching a rant, about how the whole word was topsy-turvy, helter-skelter, bassackwards. They'd heard it before, but let her go on anyway.

Molly looked up at the ceiling, at the sleek and shiny pneumatic tube delivery system. My, hadn't it always been a marvel! Once it was set up, money and messages zipped along from source to destination. It was even better than a rail system because the carriers couldn't fly off the tracks.

Oh, if only humans knew how to find the proper track to follow, flying along through curves and intersections to their proper destinations. She believed she'd traveled right with Jerry all those years, joining him at Route 66 Chapel and intending never to separate. But then he left the carrier.

Ever since his death, she has been disoriented. She couldn't depend on her children, each of them too far away and living their own lives. It wasn't that she'd gotten in the wrong path. That would be bad enough. There were no paths for her now.

It had been as if the pneumatic delivery system itself had evaporated into thin air. No wind pulled her toward happiness, and she lost the rubber and felt cushioning love had given her. If Route 66 Chapel were destroyed, she would lose faith in even the possibility of a proper journey.

Norma finally wound down in her condemnation of everything modern. Claire tapped the top of her desk and said, "Hmm. I may have something. What we'll need is headlines after the event, right?"

"Right."

"So, we can get that by doing something outrageous or by having a famous person attend the Rally. What do you think about this ... "

Claire launched into her scheme, which made both of her listeners smile broadly.

VI. Navels

At this point in the story, my daughter made an observation. "All these people trying to save a church don't seem to be particularly interested in religion."

This took me aback. Knowing how everything turns out, I hadn't realized that I'd failed to be clear about motives. But what I'd told her so far had, in fact, obscured the underlying spiritual nature of the Rescue Route 66 Chapel Campaign.

So I said to Jennifer, "A lot of us are like that. We're embarrassed to profess our beliefs out loud, but that doesn't mean we are acting out of self-interest."

"But these Fairfield citizens are getting ready to hold a public meeting. They're making the case out in the open that a building should remain a church, yet they're pretty vague about--well, say--God's presence in that place."

"Think of it this way, honey: you know how your Dad is, and he's a lot like these folks. He attends church faithfully, but he's not the kind to ask anybody else if 'Jesus is their personal savior.'"

She thought this over for a minute. "But is that a good way to embark on a quest, a mission? How will people know what you stand for if you aren't willing to explain your goals?"

This also made me pause. Had the RR66CC failed to make the case for saving this landmark in the strongest manner? I fear it came back again to the central thread holding this history together--the either/or mentality.

"Your Dad grew up in this same community. And he went to church enough as a child to endure those Bible-thumping sermons about sin and damnation. He really resented what he thought was emotional blackmail, especially for children. Being told if you don't 'come down the aisle,' you're lost forever."

"So these people you're talking about--Norma and Harry--they tend to see everyone as 'lost' or 'found,' 'blind' or 'seeing.' But they don't want to say it out loud?"

"That's right."

"We don't have that pressure, you know, in the Episcopal church. It's all pretty low-key, highly structured."

"Again, your Dad likes that, and it's the tradition I was brought up in. He hated those hell and brimstone Sundays of his youth when everyone you love must be fit into one or the other category. But he also likes to identify things and put them in clear categories"

"Well, he's not any better than his fellow Fairfieldians in expressing his beliefs."

"I think he feels he doesn't have to proclaim the faith. The *Book of Common Prayer* does it for him. As you know from your own upbringing, it's been the guide for Anglican churches around the globe for centuries. Same prayers, same liturgy--with some revision, of course, over time--from Henry VIII's day. Well, and from the Roman Catholic tradition well before that."

"My in-laws are put off by that."

"Well, we all have our individual tastes. Personally, I think there are many paths to God. What I'm trying to convey is how one group of people, whose beliefs were more internal, unspoken, were still driven by a religious impulse to preserve what they knew to be important to them and to their community."

"They should have had at least one preacher on their side. So far you've told me about a shoemaker, an insurance agent, a retired department store owner ... Come on! How are they the voice of the church?"

"Well, there is a preacher among them. He ... or she ... just hasn't acknowledged that role yet."

I knew this was a tease, hinting at some of the story's pieces I hadn't brought to the surface. But the RR66CC didn't know they had a preacher on their side either until the Route 66 Rally. And other secrets began to emerge at the same time.

Harry Blackburn's goofy infatuation with Marilyn Thomas, for instance, was now a topic for discussion among the Rally organizers. Claire expressed her suspicion based on what she happened to spy through his shop window. If she'd been able to look inside Harry's mind, she might have confirmed that desire, but not what he had determined he would do about it.

Harry was well aware that the town manager's youthful features and fit body were disturbing his previously ordered life. When she had pointed to her zippers, front and back (she was asking if he could replace them), all he saw were the round, firm moons that surrounded them. And that flesh reappeared almost nightly in dreams that made him sit up in bed, breathing heavily.

When he thought of his own aging body, Harry knew someone like Ms. Thomas would not be impressed. He was thin almost to a point of gauntness, stooped from years at his workbench, and so stiff in the mornings he felt like the tin man who needed oiling. It might be, though, that he was finally making some progress in healing his persistent itch. What a foolish malady to have, he said to himself over and over, a bellybutton rash.

He blamed this affliction on his being an innie, not an outtie, a fact he'd actually been worried enough about as a teenager to research. In that critical period of early adolescence, of course, every body feature--especially anything hidden by regular dress--is scrutinized in private to determine if it makes you more or less attractive.

In this one respect at least, the world is divided into two classes: we're all either innies or outties. More people, Harry learned, are innies. Ordinarily, the umbilical cord shrivels and withdraws after birth, producing the innie. This discovery reassured him initially; he fit into that favorite Midwestern category--normal.

When the blood supply to the umbilical cord is not completely cut off at birth, it swells and heals outward, creating an outtie. An outtie is not any more or less a problem than an innie, just an anatomical feature like a mole or big ears or long fingers.

In that trying arena of seventh grade gym class showers, though, Harry mistakenly came to an unhappy conclusion about bellybuttons. He believed that, for men, an outtie meant greater size where it mattered more, below the belly. And his innie seemed particularly small.

This adolescent anxiety gradually faded, and for decades he gave no more thought to his navel than any other man might have. He registered its functions as an unneeded lint trap, as a marker showing how our stomach muscles sag over time, as a fainter and fainter reminder of our biological origins.

But six months earlier he'd developed a mysterious rash--red, itchy, and sore around and in the navel. He tried the logical home remedies--witch hazel, over-the-counter cortisone cream, bacitracin. They calmed but did not cure the condition, which he assumed was an infection or some kind of allergic reaction.

Eventually, he consulted Dr. Sanders, a chipper young family physician only one year out of his final residence. Over the space of several months, young Frank prescribed a series of ever more potent drugs, none of which did better than had Harry's home treatment. He too assumed this was a virus or bacteria.

Finally, Dr. Sanders was forced to abandon what he had learned through the latest journals (some of them online) and pursue the kind of cure his grandmother in Cavalier, North Dakota, would have recommended. First, Harry was to bathe his navel in epson salts. Then loose clothing, washed regularly in non-allergenic soap, was ordered. Harry drew the line at herbal soaks, which he was advised to try by lying on his back and filling the innie with an eyedropper.

"You know, Doc," he said on yet one more visit, "I wonder if moisture isn't a problem."

"Moisture?"

"Yes. Here, watch this." Standing, he pointed to the tiny cavern in the middle of his tummy. He'd probably done this a dozen times before. But then he relaxed his stomach muscles. They sagged and his innie disappeared, closed up to a thin line.

"Oh!" said Frank. Always standing for examination, Harry had been tensing those muscles, unconsciously holding open his bellybutton so the doctor could see it.

"Maybe I'm trapping moisture in there, after a shower. Could it be something like a fungus?"

"Hmm. If so, my grandmother recommends a simple solution."

"I'm ready for anything simple."

"It's ridiculously straightforward: sunshine."

Still troubled about a navel that was slowly getting a suntan, Harry was nevertheless quite excited when he saw, above the low-riding pants of her exercise outfit, Marilyn Thomas' whiter bellybutton, a provocative outtie artfully displayed. The tiny gold belly ring, flattened against her tummy on one side, twinkled in his dreams.

VII. Middleman Coffee

Gene Grey declined, apologetically, to be one of the RR66CC's speakers at the upcoming rally, but he had the compelling excuse of a seriously ill friend. He and Jenny had agreed they would tell everyone the basic facts about their house guest, hoping to forestall too many questions. As a gesture of support to Molly and the others, though, he agreed to become their ombudsman.

"Our friend is very weak," Jenny explained to Norma, who was to relay the information to Claire and Molly at the next planning meeting for the rally. "I'm afraid, there's nothing to be done for him. It's, um, incurable." She wasn't going to say that Taylor's fatalistic attitude made him a difficult patient.

"That's so sad. You're too young to have to take on such a burden. Surely there's family ... ? "

Taylor's presence had added to Norma's growing curiosity about the Greys' past. Where exactly had they--and Taylor--come from? Why did the Greys choose Fairfield to locate their business? And, perhaps most puzzling of all, why did Norma feel increasingly sure that there was trouble in the marriage itself?

She knew she was treating Jenny as something like a long lost daughter, a person who'd come into her life as an adult but who'd been with her as an infant. Perhaps, nearing the actual sale of her shop and retiring to Florida, the older woman was seeking excuses to stay in Fairfield. Helping the Greys could be a reason not to leave.

"Taylor has no family," Jenny explained. "He lost his parents ... um ... in an accident, just a few years ago. An only child, we're his closest friends." In fact, Taylor never would explain his history, but Jenny had no way to seek out more information about his past.

Gene had consulted Dr. Sanders about the case, though Taylor wouldn't go see him. Later, after a tearful entreaty from Jenny, the doctor agreed to a house call. Perhaps there was some medication he could prescribe. Eventually, they would need a nurse. They put off worrying about how to pay.

Norma didn't want to pry, but she offered to help, whatever was needed. And Jenny promised to ask, but both suspected they were mostly being polite.

When Norma proposed to the RR66CC's executive committee--Claire, Molly, and Harry-- that they retire to the Middleman after the planning meeting, she said it was to thank Gene for becoming ombudsman. But Norma also wanted to continue keeping an eye on the young couple.

When they arrived, Max Bridges was having a mid-afternoon cup of coffee. Troubled by what she thought of as extreme political views, Molly had told the others that she didn't think he would want to take on an active role in the campaign. The matter had been dropped.

While they were all getting settled, Claire noticed the latest issue of *Show-Me Beacon*, a glossy magazine featuring places to see in Missouri and stories of the state's history. The Greys had copies on their reading table.

"Did any of you see this piece on Strasburg, a village 'threatened' by the meandering Osage River?" She was holding up the magazine with an aerial photo of the village on its cover.

"I did," offered Max from his table. He had skimmed the article. "That town has actually been on different sides of the river at different times. The river changed its course, taking a short cut that moved the town from one county to another." He chuckled. "Naturally, residents tried to get out of paying taxes, claiming to each revenue office that they lived in the other county."

Claire studied the magazine. "Now they say an environmental study suggests they should move the whole village to a nearby hillside. It's not very big."

"A river doesn't move," claimed Norma. "Those banks have been where they are since the beginning of time."

Max explained, "River banks are always shifting. More rain or less rain, loss of forests causing a shift in the watershed, things happening hundreds of miles away can cause a river to recede on this side, advance on the other."

"The Gasconade's always the same when I look at it," protested Norma.

"That's not what I'm interested in, though," insisted Claire. "The magazine wants to generate interest in preserving Strasburg's famous clock tower, which has a twin across the river. The river's eating at the foundation."

The town's population was divided into two main groups, one dominated by descendants of German emigrants and the other was mostly French. In the old days of steamboat travel, the two groups, on separate sides of the river (as the river was then!), had battled for control of the docks. The German clock tower was the one at which water was eating away.

Norma, studying the back cover held up by Claire, said, "Jenny, you should look at this, too. Maybe you can get the magazine to do a story on the Middleman, 'best bakery in south-central Missouri.'"

"I'll bet Claire's thinking about getting them to do a story on Route 66 Chapel, Norma," Molly explained.

Claire said, "You're right."

"There may not be enough time," Max noted. "I've heard the town is now asking for bids to take it down. They're due in three weeks, with work to start as soon as the contract is finalized."

Jenny added, "From what I've read, the *Show-Me Beacon* itself might not be around long enough for any story. I think their circulation is dwindling, and advertisers are hard to come by. I know *we* can't afford to place an ad."

"That's no surprise," Norma said. "They don't teach reading in the schools anymore--some foolish phonetic approach--and everybody gets their news off the Internet, whatever that is."

"I'd hate to see the *Beacon* go out of business," said Claire. "Look, here's another good story, about Confluence--you know where that is, less than forty miles from here. Hmm. After the last census, it's the official geographic center of America. Of the population, that is."

During this wandering discussion, Jenny had been getting coffee for everyone while worrying to herself about Taylor. Most of the RR66CC were having decaffeinated, though Norma insisted on regular. ("Never has the slightest effect on me: coffee is coffee.") Molly and Claire used cream; Harry and Max were drinking black coffee. ("Just the way it comes out of the pot," Max had said before.) Jenny herself had a latte, a double shot with cinnamon sprinkles.

Having worked her way through three years of college as a server, Jenny was good at remembering not just orders but the individual tastes of returning customers. At a breakfast joint, a take-out sandwich place, and, finally, a struggling local microbrewery, she linked regulars with their favorite requests. In some ways, her accurate categorization of customers troubled her, especially when she thought about Taylor. He just didn't fit into either the square or the round holes of her thinking.

At one point, she worried that he was an alcoholic, but, when she read up on the sickness, he didn't quite match the stereotype. Taylor didn't think of himself as morally weak, for instance; and she'd seen him take one or two drinks, then stop easily.

Because of some enigmatic statements he made about dating, Jenny wondered if he was unsure of his sexuality. But, again, what he did say often suggested he was attracted to both sexes. Was he bisexual? She couldn't place him at either end of the standard continuum.

She recognized that her new friend Norma insisted on naming and classifying everything. The owner of the Knit and Fit Shop maintained her version of the bag-tag-and-pigeonhole system by which Harry organized the Heal-All. But there was a lot Jenny didn't know about the woman who was helping her learn to knit, who was most solicitous about her personal problems, who several times seemed on the verge of some sort of confession. One moment recently Norma had stopped provocatively in mid-sentence.

"When you were young … ," Jenny had asked. "When you were still in high school, did you dream you'd leave Fairfield and travel to a completely different life somewhere else?"

"I dreamed I'd build a life right here. My parents thought I was rejecting them, but that's not really true. I just wanted to be on my own. The idea of running a business was appealing."

"I never thought I'd be so far from my parents, but there's no way I can deny that I'm rebelling. If I had to go to the other side of the globe right now, I'd do it."

"You're not so far as the other side of the globe, honey. I know where that is. It's where … it's where things happen."

Norma did not explain what far-off event she was thinking of.

VIII. Regular or Premium

When Max Bridges heard Claire say that Confluence, Missouri, stood at the geographic center of the United States' population, he announced he wanted to go there.

After the the official RR66CC business had been concluded, he asked the group if anyone would be willing to drive him to the nearby town. "I've been to the four corners of our country--even Hawaii and Alaska--but never to what we might call the exact heart of America. Unfortunately, at the moment, I have no car."

Claire was suddenly enthusiastic about a visit to Confluence "I say we make it an expedition. Have any of you seen the site itself? I haven't. It's probably one of those local places you only end up visiting when out-of-town guests show up."

"I'll go," Norma announced, pleased at a picture of herself in this tiny village near the center of the Show Me state. She would stand directly on top of a small metal plaque. Embedded in some sort of a concrete foundation, it represented the very midpoint of the country. And she thought she belonged there.

Claire asked, "Harry, won't you come? It's what ... half an hour-, forty-five minute drive?"

Harry was uncharacteristically tempted. It might distract him from his fantasies about Marilyn. (He wished he'd never seen her in that exercise outfit.) But the idea also had a strange appeal, an attraction he couldn't quite put his finger on.

The Greys were enthusiastic about seeing a regional landmark but were less sure they could get away. "We're The Middleman's entire staff, you know," Gene reminded them. Of course, he was also thinking of Taylor, who should not be left alone.

Norma suggested that perhaps Jenny needed a day off. "I think she's tired and overworked. An outing would be good for her." She put her arm around Jenny's shoulder protectively.

"Harry," Claire said, "your mini-van's the perfect vehicle. We can spread out on the three seats." Harry nodded, though he didn't say outright that he would drive.

Still, as the idea gained momentum, Claire expanded her account of the article she'd read in the *Show-Me Beacon*. The center of the nation's population, she explained, had been moving west and south since the late eighteenth century. That's when the government first began to count its citizens and when bureaucrats started to draw conclusions about our national identity from that information.

The addition of new states to the union and the later migrations of people pulled the midpoint of the country away from the East and North. The U.S. population center was first located in Maryland, then moved steadily every decade through West Virginia, Ohio, Indiana, and Illinois. Now it was halfway across Missouri, approaching mid-continent.

Molly said, "There's one more thing. I think we all need a break from the Chapel campaign before the Fairfield Prime Rally. A getaway will relax us all."

That gave Gene the excuse to say he needed more time for baking. There was so much to get ready. But Jenny could go, he said, if she wished. A college student, who'd recently asked to work part-time, could help out.

And so, it was settled: Sunday after church, they'd meet at the Heal-All and plan to be back in Fairfield by dinner time. Gene would prepare a picnic basket to take with them, samples of what he was baking in greater quantities for the rally. In some confused way, everyone was convinced this would center them for the more important campaign to follow.

That Sunday, while most of the others were in church, Harry drove out Main Street to the intersection with Interstate 44 for gas (there were no filling stations downtown anymore). He knew prices were cheapest at No Foolin' Fuelin' because they had never upgraded to pay-at-the-pump equipment. As he watched the old-fashioned rotary display count his gallons and his dollars, he calculated mentally how much he was saving by going past the Exxon, the Texaco, the Sunoco for a tankful of regular.

"Where ya' headed?" the young attendant asked as she recorded the charge without breaking the rhythm of her gum-chewing. Business was slow, and she probably assumed Harry was passing through on a long trip. Harry read the name "Judy" on her No Foolin' Fuelin' T-shirt.

"Umm, just over to Confluence."

"Confluence? Nothin' there that I know of. Family visit?" She dragged the charge machine's bar across Harry's card, pressing copies of name, number, gallons, and price into the two-sheet form with its carbon insert. "I'll need your signature."

He took out his own pen. "No. No family." He paused before signing. "You didn't know Confluence was the exact center of the United States?"

Judy gave her gum some good smacks. "That's somewhere in Kansas. Learned it in Social Studies."

"You're talking about the *geographic* midpoint," explained Harry. "Of the *continental* United States." He signed the charge slip, detached the bottom copy to fold and put in his wallet.

"Oh. And, uh, Confluence ... what's that?"

"Well, as of a recent census, the center of all the people." Harry gestured to a map of the region mounted over her right shoulder. It showed other No Foolin' Fuelin' stations in Illinois, Oklahoma, Iowa, Arkansas. She turned to look.

"If you were here ... ." He leaned across the counter and pointed to the approximate spot on the map. Confluence wasn't large enough to be identified, but no other red star indicating a No Foolin' Fuelin' appeared in the stretch of Interstate 44 between St. Louis and Joplin. He compared this to the good old days, when--according to travelers who visited his shop, at least--filling stations were all along Route 66 and attendants came out rain or shine to fill your tank with premium gasoline.

"If you were here and looked in this direction... " He pointed east, where the Interstate headed toward Confluence. "Or here ... " He pointed west, then north, and south. "Or here or here ... you would see exactly the same number of people in each direction, not counting, of course, Alaska and Hawaii."

"Ah." More smacks of Judy's gum.

"If the whole country were a flat plane," he went on, pointing, "as it is over here in Illinois, or here, north of Kansas City... And if everyone weighed the same ... you could balance all of America on the head of a pin."

July studied the map.

"You know, like angels dancing." Harry realized a bit too late that this expression wasn't likely to impress her.

"Hmp," Judy concluded and looked from the map to the window, checking to see if any more customers had driven up to the pumps.

"What we're going to do," Harry continued, for some reason unable to stop himself. He waved at the road to suggest the grandeur of this scheme. "What we're going to do is this."

Judy turned back to him, willing to listen, at least.

"We're going to drive into Confluence. Six of us. We've never been there before, not a one of us. And we'll find the marker. I'm sure they've put one up, a brass plaque in a stone or a concrete column, buried in the dirt except for the top six inches. And, and … we'll stand on it."

"Stand on it?"

"Yeah. We're going to stand right on top of the middle of the United States." Judy's eyes did widen perceptibly at this image.

"You all gonna' fit?"

He ignored her literalist interpretation. "We'll take some pictures. Then I'm going to stand there by myself. I'll lean back this way, east." He dipped to his left and forward, like the comedian whose shoes are secretly bolted to the floor. "And then I'm going to lean a little over here, toward the north."

"Hmm?"

"You see" he said with new energy and conviction. "You see, this country's lost track of where it's headed. We don't know up from down, left from right, right from wrong. We're drifting, off course. We need to get back to basics, what this nation was founded on." He thumped a fist on the counter. "So I'm going to use my weight to push us in the right directions."

"Ah."

"I know a thing or two about what's wrong with this country." Harry rocked back on his heels, one hand raised in admonition, uncharacteristically assertive. "I've seen the signs, and I know what we've been doing wrong. And I know how we can get it back to where it's supposed to be. So, I'm going to lean this way, and restore some balance. You follow me?"

Judy's face lit up with a smile. "You're going to get us all straight?"

"Exactly!"

IX. The Other Side of the Street

That afternoon the party of tourists--Claire, Norma, Molly, Jenny, and Max, with Harry driving--wound in crisp winter sunshine down the two-lane state road to Confluence. The village of only several hundred had been settled in the mid-nineteenth century by pioneering miners seeking iron ore and pyrites used in the making of sulfur. Spread along the crease of a small river valley, Confluence was banked by high hills, those flattened ridges that characterize the Ozarks.

Harry was surprised to be descending from the interstate, having thought Confluence belonged more to the flat country around St. James and Cuba he had passed on his one visit to St. Louis. He'd imagined the plaque they were looking for would be embedded in a broad stretch of mid-America. But this was rugged country, cut by winding water and featuring sharp outcrops and towering knobs. Two streams joined at the western edge of the valley and traveled along the north side of town as a single river.

"Do you see any signs?" he asked Norma, who was sitting in the front passenger seat. "Any directions to a marker?"

"I see something," said Jenny from the seat way in the back. "There's a Chamber of Commerce thingie." It was a billboard set in a small park, identifying Confluence as an Ozark river community. Canoeing and fishing were evidently major tourist attractions. Along the bottom of the sign, recently added, was the hand-lettered phrase, "Geographic Midpoint of the United States' Population."

"There it is," said Claire. "We're on the right track."

Like Fairfield, Confluence lies far from the big cities of both coasts. Rather than sharing affinities with one or the other region, such towns often stand apart as members of a third, distinctive class.

California and the other sun states had been the destinations of those fleeing the hard winters and failing industries of the rust belt. So people on the move in the '70s and '80s, rushing down Interstate 44 (formerly Route 66, "America's Highway"), had scarcely glanced at the rolling hills and scrub oak woods of south central Missouri. Confluence had begun small and stayed small.

"Now to find the actual site," said Harry, slowing so that everyone could look. In two minutes they had cruised the length of the main street.

"I don't see anything," Max noted, puzzled.

"There's got to be a place," insisted Claire. "Maybe we could ask someone?"

Harry, a reluctant traveler anyway, waited for others to direct him. Finally, he turned the mini van into the angled parking in front of a small law office, and everyone gazed at the two blocks of downtown brick stores. Claire spotted a gift shop with matching bay windows framing a double doorway, and the other women decided to go there for directions.

It was a lucky choice as the lively proprietress, Mrs. Evans, was talkative, a willing source of information about town and community. Claire also noted that they had a nice collection of postcards. She would use the cards, featuring old photos of Confluence, to commemorate their trip.

Norma knew Harry wouldn't inquire about any historic marker, the exact or symbolic spot. Like all men, he would take the illogical position that the storeowner should volunteer whatever was important to see in town. Rather than mention any commemorative marker, however, Mrs. Evans, inspired by a framed photograph on the wall Jenny asked about, told the story of a civic disaster.

"The flood of the century," the storekeeper explained, perched up on her stool behind the cash register. She was a slim woman, tall and graceful. "The nineteenth century, of course: it happened in the 1880s. Did you look at the buildings here on Main Street?"

"Well, yes," said Max. He was shuffling through postcards, apparently looking for a particular kind, as he listened to her tale.

"They're all brick. Except the tavern, right across the street." Everyone but Harry turned to look out the two wide windows. "But they didn't use to be."

"Oh?"

"At the time of the flood there were two parts of town, rich and poor. The well-to-do lived on this side of River Street, the south side. They could afford to build with brick."

"But the other side … ?" politely asked Jenny.

"They couldn't. The houses right off Main were pretty nice, though still wood. But the closer you got to the river on the north edge of town, the more ramshackle the buildings."

"And south of town?" asked Molly.

"The same folks who owned prosperous businesses and law offices and banks down here had their homes up that way." She gestured over her shoulder. "Beautiful homes right up to the hills you drove down coming into town."

"You see," their hostess went on. "You see, the flood came down the middle of Main Street, a wall of water. It took every building on the north side except the tavern. Nobody knows how it survived. All the neighboring structures were wooden. After the flood, town ordinance required that new downtown structures be made of brick."

Max stated, "I guess there was plenty of damage even in the brick buildings."

"That's right. They lost their stock, all furniture on the ground floor, furnishings. But they only had to clean up, not rebuild from scratch."

"Nobody was hurt in the flood, I hope," said Max. Harry was examining a picture he liked: a shot of Confluence in the middle of the last century taken from up high, on top of a building or perhaps the water tower. The two rows of downtown shops--one wood, one brick--balanced each other, each distinct even as the distance from the camera increased.

"Nearly a hundred people were drowned, honey. It came at night."

"What do you mean?" asked Molly, looking up from a card. "They had no warning?" Her years as an insurance agent wouldn't let her think they had not prepared for possible dangers, an alarm system to alert the townspeople.

"It had been raining for over a week. Early summer harvest. Up the valley there," she gestured to the west. "At the high end of the valley, they had been cutting hay, stacking it. But the rain began washing it downstream into the railroad trestle."

"Is this the trestle?" asked Max, shuffling the postcards again, then holding up one. Eight steel arches marched across a valley, a straight line along the top.

"No, that's a later bridge. Constructed during the buildup for World War II. That's when the mining for iron picked up again around here. The government put in that bridge. It's still there."

"Mmm."

"The old one, that's the one that gave out in the middle of the night. You see, all that hay held up by the bridge made a dam, backing up the water. It rose, and rose, and rose. Then, that night--at midnight it was--the bridge collapsed. Swept half the town away."

"Still, there should have been warning," insisted Molly. "Just watching how much rain there had been … farmers usually have some sort of gauge … or the railroad men crossing the bridge would have seen the problem and contacted their superiors. Word of mouth should have spread a warning."

"Nope. They were all in their houses, asleep. Didn't have any idea at all. It's a miracle the town was rebuilt, that Confluence didn't cease to exist."

After a pause, Claire asked, "We saw this sign," gesturing to the south. "We saw this sign about Confluence being the 'Geographic Midpoint of the United States' Population.' Do you have a marker, a commemorative site, somewhere?"

"Oh, that. No, that little sign's all we've got. For a while after the census, everybody got excited. 'Whoopee! We're at the midway point.' But after awhile, we said, 'so what?'"

Claire felt hurt, having dragged the others on what looked now like a kind of wild goose chase. "Doesn't the town want to be known for something? This makes you special."

Norma, resigned, as usual, to be the chronicler of loss, concluded, "Everywhere is turning into everywhere else."

For once Harry agreed with her. "We could have stayed home and claimed to be the center of the universe."

"Tell you what you do," Mrs. Evans said. "Go on over to the No Class Cafe, end of River Street, other side. They have wonderful pies. That'll make your trip worthwhile."

X. Angels Dancing

Before seeking out the pie and coffee, the party strolled the length of the river, now kept stable, Mrs. Evans had explained, by concrete embankments, courtesy of the Army Corps of Engineers. The town added a walking path lined with flowers and shade trees. Claire took half a dozen snapshots, attempting to create evidence that the trip had at least yielded memorable sights.

At the same time, Molly looked upstream to the west, where the flood had begun. She still couldn't believe it had not been predicted. Harry felt his usual preference for staying put in Fairfield had been justified.

Though he had inspired the trip, Max seemed more interested now that it was nearly over in watching the others than in Confluence itself. "You don't take many trips like this, do you Harry?" he asked. "Do they make you uncomfortable?"

When Norma expressed exasperation that Confluence couldn't even manage a marker, he said, "Maybe it's enough to know what you are, without advertising?"

"I'm not saying advertise. It's more labeling. You ought to know what you are and be willing to stand up for it."

At the No Class Cafe they were all startled to hear a weather forecast: winter storms for eastern Oklahoma.

"Heard it on the radio," said Ms. Hart, their large, smiling server. "It's coming tonight, maybe even early, up from Tulsa."

"I was watching the weather this morning," Claire complained, as if someone was suggesting this was another failure in her planning. "Nothing out of the ordinary for this time of year."

"They say this one caught even the meteorologists by surprise. Something about arctic cold, jet streams ... um ... tropical moisture. I don't understand those things."

Ms. Hart stood between their table and the counter. Behind her, under glass covers, were plates of sweet rolls, assorted pastry, and an array of pies.

"Who's the baker?" Jenny asked, pointing toward the display.

"That would be me," Ms. Hart admitted. Her grandmotherly figure suggested that she also enjoyed what she cooked. "But I'm just about everything here: baker, server, bus person, owner."

"You own the ... um ... No Class?"

"Funny name, ain't it. Yeah, I grew up in this very house, then converted it to a restaurant when I came back to retire."

Once everyone had a slice of pie (two apple, one cherry, two coconut creme, one lemon meringue--all delicious), Ms. Hart entertained them with her life story. Everything that had happened to her had been determined by her childhood.

"It's hard to escape your place in the family," she said. "The oldest will be an overachiever; the youngest will get babied; and the one in the middle is ignored."

Molly, a late middle-aged accident to her parents, agreed. "My parents gave me whatever I wanted. And I liked it."

Norma disagreed. "My life hasn't depended on the fact that I'm an only child."

"You can't see it," said the baker/server/owner. "I didn't for forty years. Then one day I read a book: *Caught in the Middle*. It told how the first-born and the baby of the family get their parents' attention." She looked at Molly and Norma. "But the middle child--that's me--has to act wild before anyone notices. Shoot, they used to call me a middle child, but I didn't understand how the whole thing was affecting me."

"How?" Jenny seemed particularly interested.

"Well, I run off with the circus, for one thing. I left my folks right here in Confluence forty-five … no, nearly fifty years ago. Wanted to be in the center ring under the big tent."

She pulled a chair over from a neighboring table and settled in to tell the tale.

"Then, ten years later, down in Salem, I started in on a career as a country and western singer. I was on stage in little clubs all across the land, on my way--I thought!--to Nashville, country music capital of the U.S.A."

She took a big breath. "That lasted another ten years before I realized I wasn't going nowhere."

Max nodded. "I've done a bit of that moving on myself, from one career to another."

Mrs. Hart nodded and went on. "Then I tried a series of get-rich quick schemes--real estate in Florida, futures in Chicago, California microchips. Never could get my life straight."

"Gee!" Again, Jenny was very attentive.

"Finally, I saw why I had done what I'd done: all to get attention, to impress my parents, who weren't even there to see. I got tired of being the eternal middle child, so I dropped out of the rat race and all the little cubbyholes people get stuck in. That's how the No Class Cafe came to be."

They all looked around, as if seeing for the first time the tables, the decorations, the counters. Max said, "So, it's not 'unclassy,' your place. It's that no one is squeezed into a particular class."

"That's right. Smart fella!" She smiled at him. "So, after my folks had passed on, and my sisters had moved away, I bought the family home. Fixed it up. This," she gestured, "used to be the living room. I enlarged the doorway to the dining room-- see?--and made it larger." Small portions of the old wall marked where the rooms had been divided.

"Kitchen is through that door, and I keep an office in what had been the larger downstairs bedroom. Took the smaller one for restrooms, keeping the old bathroom for the staff. Upstairs is a nice private place for me. Now I use all this to encourage everyone to avoid the roles others assign them."

Their garrulous hostess tried to convince them to stay longer, relax more, but when they saw snow flakes through the front window, they got their things together.

"You need to take more breaks like this, though," urged Ms. Hart. "I can see it in your faces. Come back now and again for dessert and coffee." They assured her they would.

Listening to the car radio on the interstate, they learned a Canadian cold air mass was bearing down on them, freezing moist winds from the South. There was going to be a blizzard.

Norma remembered riding back to Fairfield from Kansas City through a heavy snow many, many years ago. At one point after dark, she and her companion were at the top of a high hill. The road dropped gradually before them into darkness, though the lights of a few other brave travelers were visible on and off across a wide valley.

Snowflakes danced along the hood. When the wind howled, ice smashed into the windshield.

Some cars had stopped on the side of the highway. These drivers must have been more willing to stay where they were than drive farther in darkness and storm. In between swirling gusts of snow, the young Norma glimpsed smoking exhaust, as stopped drivers cut their motors on to fight the cold. Several had pulled off--or slid--at odd angles to the road. The scene resembled a long, thin junkyard, automobile hulks towed into only an approximate order.

Driving slowly and cautiously, Norma and her friend finally made it home. But the scenes from that trip had returned many times in unsettling dreams.

In one memorable nightmare, she was stopped alongside the road, snow piling up on the hood. Gazing at the growing mounds, she let her mind slip off from her body, like a soul departing.

Norma, or her spirit, floated to a point high above the scene, where she enjoyed a bird's-eye view. A long ribbon of road disappeared beneath the snow. Cars lost their grip on the highway and slid off into woods or snow banks. Travelers climbed out to call for help (making no sound Norma could hear), waving their arms and turning around to search for landmarks, bearings.

Then, in her dream, Norma floated down to the bottom of the valley and looked up to see cars and people teetering on a mountaintop. They were so far away in her (dreaming) mind's eye that their tiny forms mingled with closer snowflakes tossed and driven by the wind.

At the most frightening moment of her dream, she saw it all as a cosmic dance, angels rising to or falling from heaven. A voice spoke: "headlong themselves they threw / Down from the verge of Heav'n / … Nine dayes they fell; confounded *Chaos* roar'd, / And felt tenfold confusion in their fall / Through his wilde Anarchy, so huge a rout / Incumberd him with ruin."

She didn't recognize the words as coming from Milton's *Paradise Lost*, which she'd read at the recommendation of her twelfth grade English teacher. Satan and his followers thrown from heaven.

Norma always woke in a sweat, convinced that joy had been truly lost, that any chance at paradise was forever behind her, that this life is only a thoroughfare of woe. She couldn't know that it was soon about to change for the better.

148

Interlude: Cats and Dogs

My husband Mark claims to be a dog person. And, although he tries to be discreet about it when visiting those who have them, he dislikes cats.

"They really don't care about anything but themselves, Bella," he told me recently. I had mentioned that my secretary had kittens she was trying to find homes for. "When the kids were young, I went along with it, but not now."

Nelson was our cat person; Jenny, like her dad, loved dogs. I like both.

"Millie had them in the office today, three kittens in a shoe box."

We were on our back porch on a cool October evening. It was still before the "fall back" from daylight savings time, so we'd taken our after-dinner coffee out to enjoy the crisp air and emerging reds and yellows of a sweet Missouri autumn. I was escaping from the hardest part of writing about Route 66 Chapel, the conclusion.

When Mark asked, "What color?" I thought he might be weakening. After all, we had adopted two stray cats when the children were young: a white male we'd dubbed Oliver (after Dickens' orphan) and a black female, Scheherazade. He'd seemed to do more than tolerate them.

"Yellow. And I really like the runt, the little one." I put a warm smile behind this statement.

But Mark snorted, "Even the runts eat birds," and stood up. He peered out at the array of feeders he'd distributed around our back yard.

When we lost our last cat, Mark claimed to be happy at least that no one would be leaving disemboweled mouse carcasses on the doormat or batting a crippled bird down the garden path. And he had added several new feeders to the one we'd mounted on a pole years ago (with its ingenious collapsing baffle to thwart the squirrels). I didn't remind him that the worst case of bird eating in our family's past had not involved a cat, even though I was looking right at the scene of the crime.

His aggressive tone made me want to take on the whole notion of "dog person" versus "cat person." After all, these aren't the only choices. A good number of our acquaintances have both cats and dogs, contradicting the idea that each of us cares for only one or the other.

"Remember that vacation we took in New Mexico about three years ago?" I asked. We'd loved Santa Fe, a very pet-friendly community. They have official "dog parks," where you can unleash a pet and s/he'll find canine friends of all shapes and sizes.

"You're going to remind me of the dog-cat-mouse thing, aren't you?"

On the plaza at the heart of town, we'd seen a man walking a dog, on the back of which perched a cat, on whose back crouched a mouse. (The bottom two wore little vests so that the claws of the next animal up weren't a problem.) This traveling display was an advertisement for an animal shelter that took in the cats left on a doorstep, the dogs dumped in a ditch.

"You saw them as well as I did."

"I told you then that I believe you can train one dog to tolerate one cat, but it's hardly a natural relationship."

I recalled the discussion. We'd stepped into an ice cream parlor and were perched on stools at a small, high, round table. He had his usual double-dip cone of vanilla, and I had one dip of Rocky Road atop one of Praline Cream in a cup. (He hates it when I mix flavors.) Our discussion had become a little heated, and I probably should have quit when I was even.

But I went on. "You're right in some ways. An older dog, mature, can adapt to a kitten. And a fully grown cat can tolerate a puppy, giving her a swipe on the nose when she gets too rowdy. But maybe *people* should try things like that a bit more often. At the very least, it can be a good lesson for children."

Mark said with some energy, "Listen: there are natural enemies in the world, predators and prey.

A lot of confusion has resulted when people try to pretend we can all live in harmony."

Here in our St. Louis home, I decided I wasn't going to continue with our former argument. I'd been wrestling all day with the pieces of the Route 66 Chapel story, and I was unhappy to find myself at another of those apparent either/or dilemmas: feline versus canine, dog lover against cat lover, enemy opposed to friend. For Mark--and a lot of other Fairfieldians--it's always a choice of the Lady or the Tiger.

In calmer moments, he can see that both dog and cat are units in a much larger scheme, a system whose structure is more complex than a simple pairing of opposites. The baby wren story might make my point, but I wasn't sure now was the time to remind him of the unhappy details. We're both a bit testy these days.

We're in the process of trying to decide about our retirements, his from the highway department and mine from Western University. And sometimes our tempers seem as short as when we were getting started in life and had limited resources.

He has enough years that his pension would more than cover our current living expenses. But I stayed home when the children were young, worked part-time without those kinds of benefits, and I think it prudent to build up a bit more reserves.

Mark insists we make an abrupt and absolute division, moving together from work to retirement. He's even been looking at property down on the Lake of the Ozarks, proposing to leave the home we've lived in for over thirty years and start over. I want to ease out of one mode and into the other by stages.

It's another of those myths we take in, that in our Golden Years, we'll have settled all of life's problems. Sure, we'll have some minor health issues, the grandchildren might encounter this or that usual challenge in growing up, our children will have to make mid-career moves. But Old Age is supposed to be calm, stable, tension free; so when we encounter problems these days, we can quickly blow things out of proportion.

We were both upset at the baby wrens, he at the loss and me at the suddenness with which we discovered it.

We have a birdhouse that hangs from the eaves at one corner of our back porch, a one-hole/door affair with a ring in the roof that hooks over a nail beneath the gutter. It swings in the wind a bit, but that's never stopped wrens from nesting there.

One particularly mild and lengthy spring a few years ago, we were pleased to watch a pair of birds building their nest in the house, laying eggs, and raising their offspring. Wrens have such a melodious, trilling call that, even when we couldn't see them, we knew they were in a nearby bush or tree gathering straw or looking for bugs.

We were convinced this little house was safe from predators. No cats, we said, could swing off our tin roof to paw at it. And the big porch pillars were covered in a tough plastic siding that didn't offer sufficient purchase for even their sharp claws.

We noted with pleasure the signs of progress in wren family building: one bird sitting inside for long periods, presumably on the eggs; then weeks of parents swooping in from nearby perches with bits of food in their beaks; the small house swinging on its hook because of baby activity within; and finally little heads poking out of the door, mouths wide and calling for food.

"They'll fly soon," Mark announced one morning. "It'll probably all be over by the time we're out for coffee."

"You mean it starts at dawn, bright and early?"

"That's right. The little ones don't go all that far, to that pin oak or the big lilacs out there." He gestured toward the corner of the yard he'd made into a shade garden. "But however far they reach by nightfall, that's where they stay. They don't go back to the nest."

With our focus on cats as the killers of birds, we'd ignored another danger. The truth was hard to take in, but a different image of killer and victim now haunts our memory.

On the next morning, or the one after that, Mark told me the babies were still there. "I can see a head right now, waiting for breakfast."

He had preceded me to the porch, but once I'd settled in the swing, I checked out that baby bird. The morning light didn't reach the little house directly, so all I saw was the outline. But I noticed one thing: no wide mouth, just a pointed head.

In fact, it was as if the mouth had a worm or bug in its grasp, for I saw a wiggling there. I watched some more, but the mouth didn't open to swallow and the wiggling continued. The whole picture looked, in the silhouette I could see, less like a bird's head than something else. What?

"Mark," I said suddenly, jumping up from my swing. "That's not a bird in there." While Mark had seen cats as the enemy, he had ignored the fact that snakes eat birds as well.

Volume Three. Town Limits
Chapter 1. Adam's Apple

A few minutes past noon and ten days after the trip to Confluence, Max Bridges stood at the center of Fairfield, the intersection of Main and Eighth Streets. Less than a block to the west was Norma's Knit and Fit Shoppe. Harry's Heal-All Shoe Repair was the same distance in the opposite direction, although north of Eighth whereas Norma's store was south. On the municipal bulletin board before him was a flyer for the Fairfield Prime Rally. "Celebrate Fairfield" it proclaimed.

"This looks interesting," Max mused aloud. When he swallowed, his Adam's apple bobbed up and down in his throat, a process that had become more visible as he aged and, recently, as he'd lost weight with walking.

A voice behind him said, "I'm afraid that's going to involve a lot of wasted energy. The building's in the way of progress."

"Oh?" He turned to see beside him an attractive, composed woman, probably in her mid-thirties, pointing to the same flyer. Looking again, he saw that the rally involved organizing to save Route 66 Chapel.

"I should know," the woman beside him continued. "I'm the town manager, Ms. Thomas."

She extended a hand. "We haven't been introduced, I don't think, at least officially. I believe I've seen you walking downtown?"

"Yes. Max Bridges. Pleased to meet you."

He realized immediately that there was unusual strength in her handshake. He gestured up the street.

"I'm an addicted walker now, at least ten miles a day. But Fairfield is the kind of place where you get to know people walking. And I frequent the same establishments. I have coffee, for instance, at the Middleman most mornings and afternoons."

The Town Manager smiled pleasantly. "They've just been put under contract with the town, providing refreshments for council meetings and other events. Nice young couple."

While he hadn't been introduced to Ms. Thomas, Max could have guessed who he was talking to from the tortured description Harry Blackburn had given him. The quiet shoe repairman had tried to be casual in narrating her recent visit, but he blushed when explaining the strain that had created need for zipper repair. This woman's fitness was apparent even in her winter coat.

Max may have been recalling Harry's description of the firm body that filled tight exercise outfits, but, watching her speak, he found himself more interested in her lips. At first glance they appeared full, sensuous. But as she talked, they showed remarkably little flexibility.

"The rally might be fun anyway," he told Ms. Thomas. "There's to be some sort of 'mystery guest,' it says. I don't think I know 'Johnson's Department Store,' though."

"It's not far up Main," she gestured. "But it's been closed for a dozen years, leased now to the university for storage."

When Max heard this, he suddenly connected Carl Kendrick with the store's past. Funny, his new friend had said he'd been a businessman, but never specifically indicated what his business was. Max continued to find all these civic developments interesting, a community taking stock of its heritage.

Mrs. Evans, at the gift shop in Confluence, seemed to have had a sharp sense of her community's past, its survival from flood and subsequent rebuilding in brick. And the proprietress of the No Class Cafe believed we need regularly to step out of the boxes tradition puts us in and assess where we'd like to be.

Ms. Thomas wished Max a good day and stepped over to a black Mustang parked at the curb. (In another generally unsuccessful effort to attract customers downtown, parking meters had been disabled.) He watched her turn the key, heard the car's throaty rumble, saw her back onto the street and then drive north on Main.

As much as watching Confluence and Fairfield chart their paths into the future, Max was contemplating his own destiny on this blustery winter day. He'd had a mission coming to Fairfield, but now he wasn't quite sure how to carry it out. The story he'd heard about the Greys' young friend, Taylor, worried him. Max believes he knows who this boy is, but, if he's right, what he came to explain will be heartbreaking for more than one person.

He decided to drop by the Middleman first, and the Knit and Fit Shop later, to see what he could learn about the upcoming rally. He was willing to be distracted for the moment.

He also thought about Ms. Thomas, the town manager. Bit of a cold fish, that one. Memory of another woman, from his distant past, rises in the dark sea of memory. Maybe that's why Ms. Thomas' mouth caught his eye, recalling Penelope's.

He reached the Middleman Bakery and inspected the day's delicacies displayed in the window.

Max had not wanted to believe that the firm line of his young bride's lips revealed anything about her character, a deeper self. Nor had he ever accepted his own father's idea that Eve's bite of the apple, not Adam's, was the original sin. Max and Penelope had been so young that neither knew what the outward signs signified: his future battle of the spirit, her present one with the body.

As he reached to open the Middleman's door, Max heard his named called. Carl Kendrick, his increasingly frequent walking companion, was crossing the street behind him.

"Like some company for lunch?"

"Sure. Maybe you can tell me about this Route 66 Rally in--what?--ten days."

"Hmph," snorts Carl. "That. The women are up in arms for another lost cause. Don't waste your time."

"Odd. That's what Marilyn Thomas said."

"The town manager?"

"Right. She seems to think the building's coming down. It's already been decided."

"That would be just like Molly, Norma, my wife. They probably know their little campaign is too little too late, but they'll drag us through it anyway."

The two men settled in at a table by the window, gave Jenny their orders, and looked across the street.

Max resumed the conversation. "You'd rather spend more time at your lake house than trying to save the old stone church?"

"Not only that, but the idea of preserving the past--it's a fool's errand. The good old days are gone, if they ever really existed."

"No bright new world is possible. You've said that." He thought about the charred exterior of the old *Fairfield Mirror* building around the corner. The building might be restored or replaced, but newspapers themselves were disappearing as electronic media took over the task of providing news and entertainment to the public.

Carl has told Max about his generation's experience: inspired by the idealistic sixties but disillusioned in Vietnam and Watergate. He wasn't one of those radical hippy types, of course, but he'd been a John F. Kennedy patriot. If he hadn't already been in the military, he'd have joined the Peace Corps.

"That's another thing," Carl said once Jenny Grey had given them each their coffee, one black and one with cream no sugar. "Now the women get to go to war, and it's a good thing."

"A good thing?"

"Let 'em learn the same way I did. You see the reality of war, you won't bother about trying to change the world after that. They'll leave the guns to us and go back to knitting."

Carl held his hands over the warm cup and rubbed them together. Max studied his friend.

"You ran a business here for many years, right? A store?"

"That's right. We all have to pay the bills."

"And you never believed you were taking Fairfield into a new future, America changing and growing?"

"Oh, I was part of that. We went with plastics, we went with electronics, all the new products made cheaper with synthetic material and improved technology. Everything changes, but that doesn't mean it's getting better or worse. It's just changing, and you can't go back to what used to be."

Max finished his sandwich and wondered if he should splurge with dessert, one of these fine pastries. The habit of resisting, though, has carried over from the time when he'd had to acknowledge the first signs of middle-aged spread. He knows that now, with all the exercise and restraint of his current regimen, he's too thin. Shaving in mornings, he examines the ligaments appearing along the sides of his neck and up and down his throat. His Adam's apple is sharply delineated. He is, as his father once explained it oxymoronically, at "the youth of old age."

"Carl," he said, smiling. "I think there's something besides the Are-are-six-six-sea-sea bothering you. The rest of humanity can't be all bad, and the two of us the only good guys. Let's go for a walk and see if we can figure out what's eating at you."

II. Walking on Eggshells

In the bakery's kitchen, the Greys were talking about their house guest. Gene had slipped upstairs to find him sleeping deeply in the middle of the day.

"He's failing, isn't he?" Jenny said. "I just know he's come here to die."

"Shouldn't we try to contact someone, family?"

Gene was increasingly uncomfortable with the responsibility of keeping Taylor's situation hidden from the rest of the world.

"We promised we wouldn't until ... afterwards."

She pushed the door to the front open a crack, checking to see if Max or Carl needed anything and making sure she hadn't missed the bell above the door announcing new customers.

"Aren't we lucky," she observed when she found the front unchanged, "to be so healthy. Neither one of us has ever really been sick. And we keep in shape, just like the town manager!"

They giggled. After some recent meetings at the mayor's office, they had gotten in the habit of making jokes about Ms. Thomas' obsession with fitness, and with showing off that fitness. Though they didn't work out with any consistency, Gene and Jenny had both gone though college on varsity tennis scholarships.

"I know what you mean," Gene concluded. "We have our troubles, but we've also got the strength to deal with them. If someone's sick--not even as sick as Taylor--worry can take over their life. Health means happiness; illness unhappiness."

Wise words for someone so young. The Greys are applying a principle learned in one context (family discord versus family harmony) to another (the state of the body). They've known happiness at home versus bitter antagonism. They also sense an analogous division in society inspired by the so-called War on Terror. Is the enemy without or within?

The shop's bell announced a visitor, Dr. Sanders with his little black bag. Jenny let him into the kitchen, and then Gene escorted him up the stairs to the cot on the landing.

As she cleaned the table where Max and Carl had had lunch, she worried not just about Taylor but also about Gene. She knew how much the pressures of secrecy were bothering him.

Taylor's appearance in Fairfield and his deteriorating condition were unsettling events on their own, but he had also arrived at a crucial point in the Greys' efforts to establish the Middleman. They worried that taking care of him might detract from their ability to please customers. And they were also concerned that their new deal to supply town council refreshments might be in jeopardy after they'd been recruited by the RR66CC. If that upcoming rally were successful, the whole town might be further polarized.

Why did there always have to be two sides, thought Jenny? Couldn't she and Gene just stay neutral in town matters, cooking and delivering quality food to both conservative and progressive groups in Fairfield? OK, so Gene had agreed to be ombudsman for the Chapel supporters, but that could be viewed as in the role of a peacemaker, not an advocate.

Back in the kitchen loading plates and cups into the dishwasher, Jenny found her inner debate of the present recalling an ugly scene from the past: a war of words with her father.

"You young people can't sit on the sidelines after 9/11," he had said angrily. "That's what happened last time."

He meant with Vietnam. A career Army officer, he had never given up his belief that war protesters back home had provided aid and comfort to the enemy in Hanoi. They were disloyal citizens at best, traitors at the worst.

"Dad," Jenny had said, "we've taken out the Taliban. Al Qaeda's on the run. The Army doesn't need me. And, besides, if I went to that part of the world, I'd probably go in another capacity. Doctors Without Borders, maybe, or the International Red Cross."

That, of course, only angered him further. He argued that you had to represent your country; you had to take sides. The nation, he insisted, could not afford fence sitters.

Once, she'd foolishly tried to suggest that America's foreign policy in the Middle East and elsewhere might have been a cause of Arab anger at the U.S. Our wealth and technology plunked McDonalds in the middle of medieval villages, offered Coca-Cola in place of fine tea and coffee brewed in ancient urns, substituted loud Western music and flamboyant fashion for traditional ways.

"Don't give me any of that crap," her father had responded. "We've brought progress to those people, and they just hate our success. They hate us for being good at what we do."

She held back from mentioning the United States' support of autocratic rulers in oil-rich countries, our sale of arms to both sides in ethnic conflicts, our turning a blind eye to abuses by monarchs who cooperated with American businesses in blatant exploitation of natural resources.

Father and daughter were in a chicken-or-egg argument, taking opposing views of what had determined recent history. Did an out-of control religious fundamentalism lead to the attack on the Pentagon and World Trade Center? Or did our military and economic power leave no option but violence for oppressed peoples in other parts of the world who yearned for freedom? In rare calmer moments, each Grey suspected the other's views might--just might--have some tiny justification.

At the time of this debate Jenny was preparing to graduate with a degree in fine arts. "A worthless major," declared her father. He would have been happy only if she'd also been in ROTC. "It's a damn shame," he said, "we don't have the draft anymore. And this time it would be universal."

Jenny had heard such arguments all her life. She'd been told to resent those who used college deferments to escape military service. Nearly as offensive were families with connections that got favored sons into the Reserves or National Guard. And don't even bring up the draft dodgers and the deserters in Canada and Sweden! In his world, you were a patriot or a traitor.

Whenever she and her sister were home from college, they felt they were walking on eggshells. It took almost nothing to inspire tirades.

The bell rang out front, and Jenny pushed open the swinging doors to find the college student that Gene called "tongue-stud guy" waiting at the counter. Someone who didn't know the Greys' full story might have been surprised at Jenny's sudden change of mood. The recent frowns and inadvertent sighs vanished instantly. She looked like a person who'd hoped for something and suddenly found it before her.

"Hi, Dwayne. You're here to pick up your check, aren't you?"

He had filled in at the Middleman when she went with the others to Confluence.

"Yes, Ms. Grey." This politeness contrasted with his unorthodox dress. The tongue-stud belonged with the Grateful Dead T-shirt, painters' pants, and rope belt, but it was visible primarily because he smiled often and openly.

"I told you it's 'Jenny.' Gene's upstairs; he'll be down in a minute. Sit and have something-- something, um, on the house."

She wiped her hands on her apron and looked down into the glass cases as if surprised to find pastries displayed there. Mechanically, she began polishing the top with a towel.

"I don't have too much time. Class, you know, at 1:30."

"Oh, what class is that? What's your major. I mean, if you have a major. A lot of students don't know what they want to study for the first few years. What year are you?"

Good grief! thought Jenny. Why are you rambling on? You're the one who's older; you've nearly finished college; you're co-owner of a business. She was grateful to hear steps on the stairs that would rescue her.

Jenny might have withstood her father's bullying if her mother had come to her defense. But twenty-five years as an Army wife--moving on the average every three years--had taken away any capacity she had to oppose a Lt. Colonel. Well, that and the alcohol. In the end, Jenny concluded the only way to escape her father's demands was to disappear from his world.

She knew Gene was enduring the same pressures, though they seldom talked openly about it. They were both more comfortable when the Middleman was too busy for reflection, as it would be for the next few days. There would be extra hours of baking and packing in the evenings to prepare the rally's refreshments.

Dr. Sanders shook Gene's hand, nodded to Jenny, and passed through the shop to the street. Jenny raised her eyebrows at Gene and leaned close so he could speak confidentially.

"He says keep him comfortable right where he is. We're to contact Hospice. They can send a nurse and aides to help, if … if that's what we want."

The smiles inspired by Dwayne had left Jenny's face.

III. New Fashions

Dr. Sanders drove from the Middleman out to his office in a small complex across from the Full-mart. The giant discount center occupied five acres of concrete off Kingshighway west of town, a block and a half before it merged with Interstate 44.

Idling at a stop light, Frank mused that, in treating this young AIDS victim, he had turned into an old family doctor. Making regular house calls (on his lunch hour even!) and allowing the patient to be treated outside of the usual structure of clinic, hospital, and insurance plans was hardly what he'd anticipated in medical school and residencies. Still, the situation seemed to call for it.

At his office was the regular waiting room full of patients. Dr. Sanders employed one full-time nurse, two aides, and an office manager who choreographed the comings and goings not just of patients, but also of pharmaceutical representatives, government regulators, and insurance adjustors.

Here he could draw on the vast array of diagnostic machines, electronic databases of current medical knowledge, and the computerized records of his own practice. He referred a good number of patients to specialists simply in order to avoid later complaints he hadn't taken symptoms seriously.

Frank tried to think of each person he saw as a living, breathing fellow traveler in the human journey, but often he felt as if he worked for the Emperor in *Star Wars*, simply keeping his particular unit operational within a vast army of storm troopers. The traditional had skipped current and raced on to futuristic.

The first patient of the afternoon was Harry Blackburn, that pleasant older man with a persistent bellybutton rash. Here, at least, was an old-fashioned (and interesting) individual who seemed to think a mere family doctor could diagnose, treat, and cure his ailment. And it just might be that the home remedy from Dr. Sanders' grandmother had done the trick.

"So, how is the sunshine working?" Frank asked after glancing at Harry's chart.

"Well, I don't want to be too optimistic, after … ah, after months of trying things that didn't work. But I think it's a bit better. Here, take a look."

Harry lowered trousers and briefs about six inches, then tucked his shirttail and undershirt up under his chin, revealing his navel and a section of flat but wrinkled stomach.

"This is definitely less irritated. Very good." Frank leaned in a bit closer. "Hmm. Pull your shirt up a bit more."

It was not blocking the doctor's view, but Harry followed the instructions. "Is there something wrong?"

Frank chuckled. "Oh, no. Not at all. It's just that ... er ... you're getting a bit of suntan here. But it's limited," he gestured, "to this area here, maybe ten square inches."

The contrast was quite marked, a light brown oval surrounded by the very pale whiteness of a man who spent most of his time indoors. It looked oddly as if he'd had a transplant, as if some teenage organ donor (a lifeguard) had given him a belly patch.

"Oh, yes. Of course, I'm not removing any clothes, really. Just doing about what I'm doing here." He paused, perhaps embarrassed. "I've never done sunbathing. In fact, it's been forty-five years, I'd say, since I last went swimming down in the Little Piney. And I burn easily, so I always wore a T-shirt. So even this has come slowly."

The doctor chuckled again. "To tell you the truth, I'd been wondering where you'd find a private spot for sunbathing. You live above your shop downtown, don't you?"

Harry explained that there was an iron fire escape landing overlooking the alley off his kitchen on the second floor. The space was small, but it caught the early morning sun, and he could fit a single metal folding chair there easily. He'd been able to sit out on sunny days before his neighboring businesses were occupied or open.

"So what I do--I mean it's still winter and cold at 6:30--so I just pull my jacket, my shirt and undershirt up, my pants and shorts down. I usually get in thirty to forty-five minutes, now that I'm used to it."

Harry didn't talk about why he sometimes had to cut short his exposure, though he realized this might well be a topic other men would refer to their doctors. What had occurred first in dreams about Marilyn Thomas was now happening more and more often when he was awake. In fact, now that he thought about it with embarrassment, it had happened today in broad daylight!

Dr. Sanders declared himself pleased with the cure's progress and suggested Harry make another appointment next month. If the condition regressed, of course, he could come in anytime. Harry, covering up his unconventional suntan, expressed his gratitude. For a moment he considered discussing the other effect of his treatment, but shyness made him put that off for another visit.

Decades ago Harry had officially labeled himself "celibate." Even if it wasn't by choice, carnal pleasure had disappeared from his life. Like a medieval monk he'd found he was able to banish the thoughts that stirred up a desire he'd known intensely in adolescence. And what had been occasional bouts of frustration became more and more rare.

Only recently had he considered moving himself to an opposing state, the most recent name for which--"sexually active"--he'd learned by reading *People*. The magazine article, chronicling current trends, was describing both teenagers and seniors. Perhaps if Marilyn Thomas hadn't come to town and inspired his odd dreams, he would not even have noted the term. Now, given both his recent nighttime and daytime experiences, he wondered in what group he should be categorized.

Through his early twenties Harry had hoarded a handful of imitation *Playboy* magazines he'd found sticking out of a drug store trash can. Perhaps once a month he studied a favorite picture sequence: a shoe salesman who looked like Gary Grant seduces, in a triple-mirrored dressing room, the woman who manages the lingerie department. Now, years later, the underwear salesperson's face (in Harry's daydream), seen from three different angles, is the new town manager's. Well, they have pretty similar bodies, too.

Harry suspected what he was tempted to complete on the fire escape landing wouldn't exactly fit *People*'s definition of "sexually active." Still, it was a sharp departure from what he believed characterized his personal life.

The recent reemergence of something like lust was so unexpected, especially after years of abstinence, that he couldn't find any way to discuss the subject with this young, pleasant, and clearly well-intentioned physician. But he did have questions.

In the waiting room, Harry had noticed a discreet Viagra brochure. He was alone, as the office manager had disappeared from her little window. So he took one and quickly folded it into a size small enough to fit in his hip pocket.

He had plenty of evidence that his machinery was still functional in isolation. But remembering a number of youthful embarrassments, he wondered if all would be operational in a situation of genuine intimacy. Perhaps he should have a back-up, an insurance policy of sorts.

The man pictured on the brochure was younger and more attractive than Harry, and the woman who smiled gratefully at her companion would have been out of place in the Heal-All Shoe Repair Shop. But Harry found the romantic picture alluring.

Driving back to his shop, he blushed, recalling this morning's episode.

The temperature had been just above freezing, warm for the time of year. Taking his morning coffee with him into the sunshine, and well wrapped in coat, scarf, gloves and hat, Harry soon felt almost toasty on the black metal landing. He knew he'd have to fight a tendency to drift back into comfortable sleep.

He let his mind wander to childhood, boyhood, early manhood. He moved from a neighborhood game of tag through a playground session of flies-and-grounders to a scene of unexpected and quirky romance he'd repressed the rest of his life. Why was she doing that?

A cool breeze wound through the fire escape's railing and tickled the few small gray hairs on his tummy. His imagination (or was it part memory?) pictured a woman's head, a face, a mouth with lips preparing to … could it be to … to whistle?

The breeze became stronger, colder, more intense. It shot down across his bellybutton and dove deeper, as if a hand were reaching.

And then an irritating voice said, "Harry Blackburn, you crazy old bachelor, what are you doing up there?" Standing in the alley below him was his familiar antagonist, Norma White.

"Harry," she said, "I need your help … again."

IV. Flies and Grounders

Jerked out of his early morning fantasy into a state of panicked alertness, Harry tried to concentrate on the here and now. He was lucky not to loose control of his coffee cup and drop it on Norma's head.

"I'm ... it's ... there's ... just getting some air." Afraid to adjust his clothes with her watching, he was frozen in place.

"You look like you slept in your clothes on the landing."

Harry rallied. "It's where I often, on sunny days, come to, um, have my coffee." Still sitting stiffly, he raised his cup.

Harry knew this alley was used as a shortcut for pedestrians on their way to or from the municipal parking lot by the old train station. But foot traffic before businesses opened was rare.

"Come let me in," Norma demanded and started off in the direction of the gap between the bank and Prescott's law office that would take her out to Main. Then she would come around the corner and down Eighth to the front of his store.

As Norma strode purposely away, Harry at last rose, straightening his clothes. He called after her, "What do you mean,"he called, "you need my help?"

She did not respond until they were both inside. He'd left coat and hat upstairs, double-checking that his pants were zipped and buttoned. He smiled with satisfaction that the key element in his erotic daydream had not wilted immediately at Norma's appearance. He found her sitting on one of his auditorium seats with a coat folded across her knees. He perched on his work stool.

"Harry, I'm very close to selling my store and moving to Florida. There. What do you think of that?"

He was surprised, but also puzzled. "That's fine. Do you have to consult anyone about this?"

"In other words, you don't care?"

Harry stopped to think, knowing something was expected of him. "You don't have to stay in Fairfield ... for me. Or just because you were born and raised here."

"Oh, you're as dense as ever, Harry!" She moved her coat off her lap in an angry gesture, shook it out, and draped it across her knees again, frowning at the paper bags of repaired shoes, purses, harnesses on the shelves along the back wall.

Why, thought Harry, are women so emotional? What does it matter, really, if she does what lots of people our age do? Sell and find a nice place in a warm climate to live out their days. She's got no family here. Why not go south?

Men, he reasoned, approach such situations logically, first adding up the pros and cons, then arriving at decisions through a series of questions and answers. She's thinking people's feelings will be hurt, or that her friends--Claire and Molly--will be disappointed. That doesn't matter.

He connected the state of her store to emotional confusion: no neat filing system, imprecise inventory, prices subject to negotiation. His own rates were printed on sheets of paper taped to the front door and his counter by the cash register. And, of course, his filing system was impeccable.

Still, he had to admit that men sometimes did things that might not seem logical to women because they lived in such a different way. He remembered a confrontation with Norma many years ago, when they were both teenagers. Their different perspectives had underscored other divisions of childhood.

She had been walking by his house on her way home after working a Saturday morning at Minnie Miller's Knit and Fit Shop. He was bouncing a tennis ball off the porch steps, a common pastime for boys with no one else to play with.

"What are you doing, Harry?" she'd asked. He didn't see how she could not know.

"Practicing." He threw the ball so that it hit just below the bottom step, bounced up into the front of that step, and then then came back to him at a forty-five degree angle from the sidewalk. He caught it on the fly in his gloved hand.

"Practicing what?"

He froze with his arm cocking in the throwing position and looked at her in frustration. Surely he didn't have to say this was how you improved your baseball skills, your timing and hand-eye coordination for games like flies-and-grounders? Didn't everyone know this? Without answering, he threw the ball again, imperfectly this time so that it hit a step's edge and skidded along the sidewalk. Still, he stopped it with his glove, imagining himself a Golden Glove winning shortstop.

"Why aren't you down at the park, playing with the other boys?" Green Acres Park was just two blocks away, and Norma was right that on a Saturday there would be pickup games there.

"I'll be down there later. I've … um … I have to stay around until my Mom comes back from the store."

The truth was Harry wasn't that good at baseball, one of the last to be chosen for a team. The captains (voted to that post by the others) would make him bat ninth and play right field. At school he hadn't even tried out for the sport after his first failure, in seventh grade, to make an initial cut.

Still, this was how men operated, he knew, with a clear system, a recognized order, no emotional muddying of the water. You were ranked precisely by your ability. Women, on the other hand, would want to give every player who tried the same chance to play. They would distribute praise to the weak players as well as the strong. They might not even keep score.Looking at Norma many decades later, Harry confirmed his opinion that men and women were on different sides of a divide.

He could imagine there being no more Fit and Knit Shop, no Norma White in Fairfield. Just as easily, he could see her giving up the building to Farmtown Industries but living pretty much her same life in the only town she'd ever known. It was all a matter of deciding what you wanted. No one else need be consulted.

Would there also be a day when the Heal-All closed? It's true he'd never thought very seriously about the time when he would no longer want or need to work. That was a bridge to be crossed in the future. But then again, he'd also assumed he'd never have to decide what to do about early morning evidence of physical desire.

Norma sighed. "That's not what's really troubling me."

"Oh?" He was still finding it hard to believe she wanted to confide in him rather than, say, Molly or Claire.

She went on. "I find I'm ... I don't know, haunted. Haunted by pictures of the past, of ... you know."

Harry at first assumed she meant Robbie White, her high school boyfriend and, later, a fallen hero in war. How could he help her with that ghost? He was surprised, though, at a further unexpected turn in her thoughts.

"Have you seen that boy, that young man, Jenny and Gene are taking care of? Taylor, I guess his name is."

"No, he's been upstairs, in bed, I think."

"Yes, most of the time. But one evening Jenny let me carry some soup I made up to him." Norma paused, a faraway look in her eyes. "He's very good looking, that boy, except so thin. Still, his face, it's striking, handsome when he, when he smiles."

Harry was at a loss. He felt sorry for anyone who was ill. And apparently this boy was dying. But he didn't know him, didn't see why his case should be compelling to Norma. And he didn't understand why Norma had chosen him as confidante. Weren't they, after all, lifetime antagonists, political opposites, believers in different goals?

"Look, Norma." Harry was willing to state the case as he saw it, if for no other reason than to end the discussion. "We've each got to make our own decisions. You can stay or move, whatever you want."

"Honestly, Harry, you make things sound so … so matter of fact. Move or stay, come or go, live or die. It's not all the same, you know." She rose to put on her coat.

Although he'll never admit it to Norma, even flies and grounders could be confused. The low line drive might actually be fielded as a one-hopper. The batter couldn't always tell from the distance what the other player had, 50 points or 100.

In his mind, Harry compared the woman he saw before him and Marilyn Thomas. They, surely, were not the same. One, his contemporary, suffers the inevitable process of aging--new wrinkles, extra weight, weakened senses of sight and hearing. The other, young enough to feel her life was really just beginning, her faculties at their peak, her body honed with precision, her mind in command of her own destiny.

"Norma," he said, surprised at his own thought. "I don't know what you're going to do, but you've inspired me to a decision. I'm going to ask someone out on a date!"

V. Out and Back

Norma left the Heal-All, conceding to herself that she should have sought advice from her women friends rather than from a "confirmed bachelor." Late that afternoon, meeting Claire and Molly at Johnson's old store for a final review of Rally plans, she confessed her plight to them.

Molly was hurt. "It's not just that we need you for the campaign, but you're one of our oldest friends. Especially after ... " She was going to say "after I lost Jerry," but she knew that was unfair. "Especially if we lose the chapel, I don't want you to be gone, too."

Claire said, "You might sell the shop, but you could still help me with the Antique Store, part-time maybe. I'm really committed this time. And I've come up with the name: 'Past Presents.' Kind of a play on words, you see? It brings things from yesterday up to now and takes us back to bygone days."

Norma assured them both that she hadn't made up her mind, only that such a good offer was tempting. And she didn't, in the end, know if Horatio Radar and Farmtown, Inc. were behind the deal. Perhaps it would turn out that the couple from Kansas City making the offer simply saw her store as a good place for a small business. In the end, she assured them she would be here for the Rally and some months after that, so they could talk more.

Claire was also hoping Norma would remain to make sure the Rally was a success. She'd become convinced the building they were in--in some ways, an analog of Route 66 Chapel--was important to that effort.

"But I still have my reservations about what you're going to do at the Rally," said Norma. "It's a little bit dishonest."

"Well, we have to get around the mayor's refusal to let us have our event at the Chapel," said Molly. "And we'll do everything we say on our flyers, beginning with a call for a return to Fairfield Prime."

"Doesn't the store look good again?" asked Claire, swinging an arm at the effect. After the university had moved out what it had in storage, she hired a cleaning crew . The old black-and-white tile floor was bright, the octopus/Big O's chrome pneumatic tubes and their fixtures shone in fluorescent light, and stark shapes of molding and trim framed doors and windows.

"It does," Molly agreed. "I'm bringing the photo exhibit of Fairfield designs tomorrow. My secretary had Kinko's make those giant posters, thirty-six inches high. And you can get easy-to-use cardboard exhibits ... oh, everywhere." (She didn't want to admit her secretary had found them at Full-mart.)

Making these preparations, Molly and Claire had found their goals evolving. They now felt that Route 66 Chapel was not the only thing that should be saved. All Fairfield's remaining old buildings deserved preservation, and especially Johnson's, which was becoming linked in their minds to the stone church.

While the interior of the store had been redecorated in the late 1950s, and the Chapel's had not, they were both about the same age, early buildings in Fairfield's history. The store's bricks had been locally produced by The Osage Fire Brick Company, a well-known, turn-of-the-century operation near Jefferson City. The facing on Johnson's building also featured several panels of Ozark giraffe matching the church's exterior.

One institution was designed for prayer and religious services, important to the spiritual life of the community. But the other was also crucial to the town's functioning as the place (once the "general" store) where essential material goods were found. When times were hard, not long after the town's beginning and later during the Depression, the barter system had been used freely, a dozen eggs exchanged for roofing material.

Above all, Johnson's pneumatic tube delivery system, connecting the departments of the store to a central office, recalled for these women a unified, integrated, communal life. The machinery, they thought, was like the body's circulatory system, bringing life to limbs and to the heart itself.

"I'll tell you something else," Molly had observed before Norma arrived. They were reviewing the final list of refreshments sent over by Jenny. "But you can't tell Norma."

Claire was surprised. "What do you mean?"

Molly smiled broadly and explained. "You know how you can't mention highways--or roads or streets--without her complaining about three-lane Route 66."

"Of course! It should be either two or four lanes."

"Well, this tube delivery system is just like a good road system, linking up friends, relatives, even people who don't know each other in one structure. The number of lanes doesn't matter."

"Ever hear that old story about the Chapel's services? About the collection?"

"That they passed the plate down the aisle to the minister and then back again?"

"Yes. Do you know why they did that? Or at least, this is what I remember. Even though the collection was a gift to God, and the minister was supposed to receive it for God and His work through the church, Reverend Emerson didn't think it should stay with him."

"So he sent it back, but where? To the ushers."

"To a little table off to the side, near the entrance. But the funny thing is, it had to go up and down each aisle a second time. So everyone in the church saw it coming and going."

"Of course, finally there weren't enough hands to give or take. They all passed on, the congregation, from this life to the next. I never really thought about the church's passing at the time, did you?"

"No, not really. I guess we were going to our own churches." (She was Baptist; Molly, Methodist.) "It's sad really."

Both sighed with a vague sense of having failed somehow, not intentionally but through a loss of attention, a self-centeredness that had seemed appropriate at the time. Now a related regret was fueling their commitment to the RR66CC.

Reviewing with Norma the sequence of events Molly had drawn up, Claire pronounced her satisfaction at their own efforts to this point. She asked the other women, "Will the Greys be ready?"

Norma responded, "Oh, yes, Even with their ... their sick friend, they say they're on schedule preparing refreshments."

"The flyers have been up for a week, and there have been radio announcements. Speculation about the Guest Celebrity is helping. The latest rumor is that it's some sort of Hollywood movie star."

"We still need to be sure there will be enough men," Norma noted. "Harry will be there."

Molly turned to Claire. "Carl?"

"Carl … oh, Carl's gone to our lake house. We won't be able to count on him."

Molly clucked her tongue, thinking to herself that Claire shouldn't have let him go. If she had to … if she were his wife, she would go after him. Jerry wouldn't have had to be coerced, she's sure. Would Max have gone with Carl?

If Claire suspected unspoken criticism in Molly's question, or was unhappy at Carl's not helping, she showed no sign. The crisp, clean interior of what would soon be "Past Presents" was giving her too much pleasure. She was particularly pleased that she had found the tube delivery system, her father's octopus, still functional. The same man who worked on her church's organ had performed some minor repairs on the blower, but that was it.

Her gaze swept across the store's interior, and she envisioned refinished old furniture in this section, fine antique china and glass here, inexpensive but valued memorabilia along the far wall. She imagined stopping by garage sales and looking out for auctions where she could build her stock.

It was good to be busy again, or busier at least. When she'd worked at the store, after the children were in college, she'd been surprised that she enjoyed the ritual of coming to work every day. A stay-at-home mom for over two decades, she'd adapted to an irregular schedule of trips to the grocery store, schools, meetings. She had no sense of "at work" and "off," for she was on duty, as the kids say now, "twenty-four/seven."

`She had to admit, to herself if not to her friends, that the old dichotomy of masculine and feminine roles could sometimes be blurred. The pneumatic cartridge, she thought, containing money headed to the cashier, was the same as the cartridge returning with receipt and change, just headed in an opposite direction. The tubes were "in" and "out," but the carriers were unchanged. Function defined identity, not some intrinsic core.

What was that she saw through the front window? Wasn't that the young man--what was his name?--the Greys were taking care of? He was thin, bent over, moving so slowly. Should he be out by himself? Where was he going?

VI. Inner Light

At this point my daughter Jennifer interrupted the telling of the RR66CC's campaign. "Wait a minute, wait a minute! You've got too many mysteries here: what's Taylor running from; who, really, is this Max guy; what's the RR66CC's secret Rally plan; who's behind Farmtown, Inc.; an unknown celebrity?"

I had to laugh because she was right. But I hadn't planned to hide the answers to these questions. I was just trying to describe the principal players in this little drama first, then follow events more or less in chronological order.

"I'm sorry," I said. "I didn't mean to be mysterious. It's just that you need to understand how these would-be chapel rescuers saw things. They were in the dark just like you are."

"Not all of them. I mean, don't Molly, Claire, and Norma have a plan for the Rally?"

"Yes, that's true. But you know perfectly well that events don't always follow the plans we draw up for them. And there were surprises in store for the organizers. Don't forget that the mayor and Ms. Thomas had been working as hard to block the campaign as the RR66CC labored to set things in motion. They, after all, were very interested parties who stood to profit from this deal."

It was a classic little guy versus big guy story, I realized once more. On one side were regular citizens with no experience in political action. And opposing them was a third-generation mayor who had put in with out-of-town money, joining a group that had won several battles like this already.

I suppose that's another reason I was drawn to the Fairfield story in the first place. I'd never been a big time player, even when I was mostly at home raising my children. And at Western University, where I had become Director of Counseling, I still tended to concentrate on helping my clients. Deans and vice-presidents made the policy I worked within; and I seldom challenged the system. That's one of the reasons I am semiretired to private practice.

But my little group of Route 66 rebels was saying it wouldn't go quietly into the night. If, in the end, they lost, at least the other side would know they'd had a fight. Yea for them!

One of the things they had not adequately foreseen, though, was the role Max Bridges would play. A newcomer to the community, he had been a passive figure to this point. Patronizing shops popular with the older crowd and listening to stories about Fairfield's past, he offered almost nothing about his own history. And he had found an important source in Claire's husband.

I said to Jennifer, "Let me tell you about Carl for a moment. Remember he had gone off to his lake cottage?"

She interrupted. "After he insisted to Max that women should serve in combat." I knew any issue involving gender roles would catch her attention.

"Very good. I thought you'd recall his proposal. But that wasn't what he was most concerned with. Retirement allowed worries he'd buried for years to surface. He was a troubled man."

"Well," admitted Jennifer, "you, longtime counselor, understand that. Was he clinically depressed?"

"Perhaps he was. Of course, I can't say exactly who ... um ... became my client, but I did get to know him."

"He came all the way from Fairfield?"

"Some Fairfield people were referred to me by a friend there, Dr. Hodges, who thought they might open up with someone not in the community."

"Was this post traumatic stress disorder? The Vietnam War."

I didn't want to get into such detail, so I said, "Back up a minute and recall that Carl was being counseled by Max informally, on those walks about town. Max had, it turns out, some experience working in this area, as a minister."

Jennifer's eyes opened wide at this. "A minister? Ah, at last, the religious theme in the tale of one old church."

"Well, technically his title wasn't 'minister.' And, of course, he was never at the chapel, whose last parishioner had been dead decades before he saw the little stone building on one of his early strolls about town. But he was indeed a religious leader who'd served--and served well--in several churches."

"He seems so far to be someone on an extended vacation, or someone who's dropped out, or ... " She giggled, as if she were now the one hinting at secrets in this history. "Maybe he's in a witness protection program!"

"That would be a good twist, wouldn't it! Actually, he'd asked for an extended leave from his church, with the hope of helping a dying friend."

"OK, let's get down to facts here. What's his story?"

"I'm about to tell you that because everyone in Fairfield began to learn about him at the Rally. He was a Quaker clerk, the one who directs their meetings."

"That's right," Jennifer agreed. "Quakers are very democratic, so there's no official minister in charge."

"Yes. As I understand it, congregations try to come to a consensus on any action."

"That's certainly unusual for our time. You can't get two opposing sides agreeing on any joint resolution! But haven't the Quakers been progressive? I know they're opposed to war."

"They were also leaders in efforts to end the separation between white and black, segregation."

"Hmm. There's not much of a structure or liturgy to the service, is there?"

"I believe that's right, very unlike our Episcopal service."

"Still, the Church of England is famous for it's 'middle way,' trying to avoid extremes on any issue. We sometimes even bridge the divide between Catholic and Protestant."

"Well, Quakers go about their work without a lot of fanfare. Just good works, tolerance, an opposition to open conflict. And lay people really do run the church, not bishops."

"What about services at Route 66 Chapel. I mean, the circuitous path of the collection plates is interesting. It sounds as if it's part of a philosophy-- or, I guess, a theology."

"It's sad," I explained, "but no one in Fairfield seems able to recall more than scattered incidents and rumored practices to define this church."

"Maybe they relied on inspiration or revelation. You don't need a complex structure for that. Isn't that also central to Quaker thought?"

"An 'inner light,' yes. Not formal dogma or the workings of hierarchy. The way will come from those with spiritual insight and separation from material desire."

"So, all these people--Molly, Claire, Norma, Harry--were determined to save a church without any particular commitment to its history or knowledge of its principles?"

"Well, I wouldn't say no commitment. They didn't know the details, the specific articles of faith. But they knew faith was important, and it seems the chapel's unorthodox character allowed citizens from different churches to unite in one cause."

"It still sounds vague, a quest for a Holy Grail that no one's really seen."

Jennifer's offhand observation stayed with me. "A Holy Grail that no one's really seen." How many of us are chasing hopes that originate in dreams, not in reality? Since none of us is ever completely satisfied--in this life, at least--is what would make us feel whole an illusion, a myth we accept from our ancestors or the culture that surrounds us?

This conviction that future possession of a certain material object, or achievement of some rank, or conquest over a recognized enemy will give us peace may be connected to the universal phenomenon of nostalgia. There was a time, we all believe, when we had things exactly the way we want them. Once in humankind's past (perhaps long, long ago) the world was as it should be. We understood good and evil, white and black, whole and broken.

Maybe the tenets of the Route 66 congregation were lost to the present generation, but the desire for an unshakable faith still animated countless souls. And they knew too much about their own churches' weaknesses and failures to believe absolutely in those establishments.

It's true that the Route 66 building had fallen from an ideal state, back when faithful parishioners repaired cracks in the Ozark giraffe facing, regularly polished the floors, the pulpit, and the pews, and made sure the foundation was kept dry by open gutters and carefully placed down spouts. That didn't mean what remained had to be torn down, carted away, plowed under.

Perhaps the goal of the RR66CC was the principle of salvation itself. However imperfect we are or the structures that support us are, we have to believe that what we value can be restored, retained, rescued--even from forces we do not understand.

VII. Odd Couples

Johnson's Department Store was full of people. Some wanted to tour the building, which had been closed to the public for ten years, and see a demonstration of the "restored" pneumatic delivery system. Others were drawn to the cause itself, historic preservation. Everyone wondered about the "national celebrity."

Claire was particularly pleased at one last-minute attraction Molly had devised: door prizes. Everyone who came received a flyer with a tear-off entry slip. Jenny Grey had agreed to draw the winning slips from a glass bowl. Molly wouldn't identify the prizes except to say that they would be mementoes of Fairfield in the 1950s.

Norma remained cynical about the Rally's chances for success, but she had helped Jenny arrange the little tuna, beef, and chicken sandwiches, spinach mini-quiches, assorted pastry desserts and cookies. She hadn't been told about Taylor's recent disappearances.

No one had more information about Farmtown, Inc., the mysterious corporation that wanted to buy downtown and, according to one story at least, plow under all its buildings. Max had proposed the most logical theory, that what was intended was a major industrial park. Farmtown,

Inc. would probably turn out to be a manufacturer of agricultural equipment.

"Why is *she* here?" Norma asked her young friend, pointing to Marilyn Thomas. "She wants to raze Route 66 Chapel."

Jenny said, "It's a civic event, I guess. I'll be surprised if the mayor himself doesn't show up, pressing palms and slapping backs. Oh, hi, Mr. Blackburn."

Harry ducked his head in response and nodded at Norma. She wondered if he was here because the new town manager was. That was Molly's theory, but if ever two people didn't belong together, Norma thought, it's this skinny old shoemaker and the young woman who had to be shoehorned into her slacks!

To Norma's way of thinking, there were other odd couples in the store. There's that Max Bridges steering Molly by an elbow off to one side. We don't even know where he's from, yet she's the heart and soul of central Missouri traditions.

Who was Claire talking to, one of the college students? She should be relaxing with her husband in retirement at Lake of the Ozarks, not chitchatting with a boy one third her age who sported a chunk of metal in his mouth (not, of course, braces to straighten teeth!).

Norma would never admit it, but her noting of odd couples is neatly contradicted by the effective balance of differences in Fairfield Prime (especially black and white), the basic design feature of Johnson's Department Store: the checkerboard tile floor, the black frames around white door and windows, black wainscoting and chair rail around the walls.

Molly moved away from Max to the platform on which the old office had been located. It's walls had been taken down, so it was a small open stage. Molly stepped to a podium, borrowed by Claire from her church Sunday school. Above her the Big O's tubes come together from the store's former stations: clothing, house wares, linen, candy, cosmetics. Molly stands where the store manager used to sit to receive payment and send change.

"Could I have your attention, please," Molly began. She and Claire would make a brief presentation about Fairfield's past and then ask for support in the effort to rescue Route 66 Chapel.

"Thank you all for coming this afternoon. Before I explain in more detail why we're here, please direct your attention to one of the co-owners of The Middleman Baker, Jenny Grey." She pointed to the back of the store, where Jenny made a shy wave. "She's going to draw a number out of her glass jar, and we'll award our first door prize."

Perhaps half of those present glanced at the flyer they held to check the number printed there. Rather than read out the winner, Jenny put the slip of paper in one of the Octopus's cartridges. She flipped open the lid of a tube on the wall behind her (once the kitchenware station) and snapped it shut. All eyes followed the route of the tube, though they couldn't see the cartridge itself, which announced its arrival beside Claire with a light chiming sound: *ping*. The cartridge's passing depressed a mechanism, which, when released, rang the bell.

Molly read the number, and Sam Jensen, who'd delivered the mail to the oldest neighborhoods in Fairfield for years, received a receipt holder used in Johnson's Store. It's a bright spike on a solid brass base onto which paid tickets were speared. Two more prizes would be given out during the Rally.

After light applause, Molly began to explain how her fellow citizens had a chance to preserve a special Fairfield trait: economically taking advantage of local resources. While she spoke, old Harry, with his hidden tanned tummy, worked to position himself close to the sexy town manager. He saw her muscular thighs, behind, and back accented by a tight outfit.

Jenny, happy that attention had turned away from her, noticed Gene entering the store with more trays of pastry. Even at this distance, though, she could see he was distressed. What now? Taylor gone again?

"Take Ozark Giraffe," Molly said. "Central Missouri's hills are full of limestone that can be easily carved to make walls and facings. So you see in town and across the countryside houses, stores, and sheds whose walls represent our state's geographic identity. Do we want to lose our distinctive character?"

Norma snorted to see Harry eying Marilyn Thomas's physique. And now Claire's husband came through the store's back door near Jenny. Wasn't he supposed to be at the Lake? Is he looking for Claire or his friend Max?

"But we're not just talking about saving material resources," Molly continued. "These old buildings are expressions of people who settled here originally, and those who've moved here in later times. In the 1950s local residents developed a style which eventually earned the name of 'Fairfield Prime.' It's clean lines and stark contrasts reflected our fitting in the scientific successes of the Space Age."

In order to give time for these truths to sink in, Molly asked Jenny to send up the number of a second winner. A walnut coat rack went to one of the university's secretaries. It had stood for years, she explained, in the store's office.

After putting out the extra pastries, Gene came to stand beside Jenny. He leaned over and whispered into her ear. Norma, who had kept her eye on her young friend, watched Jenny's eyes widen and her face take on a look of concern. She whispered questions to Gene, but he shrugged his shoulders and shook his head sadly.

Meanwhile, Molly began to advocate a return to basics, to the values of that period after World War II and before the revolutionary 1960s. Back then, she claimed, everyone and everything had a place and a known identity. And it was clear she felt this clarity came with a sense of purpose, the pursuit of America's greatness. "If the buildings that feature Prime are gone, we'll forget our past. We'll no longer know who we are."

Norma saw Carl try to get Claire's attention. His wife was standing behind and to one side of Molly, an assistant in this presentation. She arched her eyebrows--what does he want?

More startling to the owner of the Knit and Fit was Harry's inching closer and closer to Ms. Thomas. She seemed completely unaware of his presence, but his elbow was nearly rubbing hers.

Unexpectedly, Molly lost the thread of her argument. She'd been about to conclude that clear identities and known goals give direction to a community. And she was going to remind her audience that opposites and contrasts are necessary to meaning. But she realized how very politically incorrect she was sounding.

In her heart of hearts, she wanted to say that nowadays we don't know up from down, left from right, men from women, ally from enemy. And that's why we have to restore old values by preserving old buildings. But the voices of her grown children, the media culture of the present, and even a growing awareness of this idea's limitations are cautioning her not to make that the final justification for the RR66CC.

"Jenny," she calls brightly. "Give us one more winner before I announce the surprise Phase II of today's Rally."

Norma, watching Jenny insert the slip into another cartridge, can tell her young friend is still upset by what Gene has told her. Norma frowns when Ms. Thomas finds herself the winner, though stepping up to take her prize moves her away from Harry. The town manager receives a sewing form, the wire shape of a woman's torso on which clothes could be fitted.

"Now," announces Molly. "We're going to move our Rally to the grounds of one of Fairfield's most historic buildings: the mayor's house. There we'll be greeted by our surprise celebrity."

VIII. Pivotal Moments

The Paterson house, originally built before the Civil War, had been purchased by the current mayor's grandfather, himself a mayor, early in the twentieth century. It's grand structure reflected two phases of Fairfield history. And now, if the RR66CC had its way, it would become the site where a third phase began.

As Molly led her friends through the doors of Johnson's Department Store and out onto Main Street, her mind raced to find a way to conclude her argument. A return to Fairfield Prime *must* be good for all citizens. She was mildly irritated to find Max walking beside her, apparently intent on opening a conversation.

Originally, Molly had thought the continuation of the Rally in front of the mayor's house would primarily serve a political end--identifying Paterson as the foe of historic preservation rather than the wise leader promoting economic development. That label of anti-tradition was to be accentuated by the irony of his occupying one of the town's famous landmarks.

As at least half of the Rally participants followed along the three-block walk to Missouri Avenue, Molly realized she could do even more with the help of her mystery guest. She could make

Paterson pay a personal price if he refused to help her cause. What Molly wants to establish is a kind of quid pro quo. If she and her friends lose Route 66 Chapel, the mayor has to give up his house. She's knows it's a stretch, but the notion isn't completely indefensible.

Among those following Molly on the street, but not endorsing her cause, was Marilyn Thomas. This surprised a number of people, including her would-be suitor, Harry. He assumed Ms. Thomas wouldn't want to be seen by her boss protesting his policies on his own front lawn. Still, the trek to Missouri Street might be just the chance he's been looking for to ask the new town manger out. Seeing her shoes land and lift on the sidewalk, he wonders: is she truly a toe-first walker (and therefore a kindred spirit)?

The mayor's house, once known as the Stone Mansion, was built before Fairfield's founding. Rupert Stone, an early railroad engineer, helped develop the line eventually linking St. Louis and points east with the American Southwest and San Francisco. His expansive frame home, occupying an entire block in the newly created Fairfield of 1860, underscored the town's identity as a railroad center.

When the second Mayor Paterson inherited the Stone home from his father in the 1930s, he redecorated it with a highway theme in honor of Route 66. In addition to commissioning quirky paintings of roadways, automobiles, and celebrity travelers who had toured the Mother Road, he replaced wood siding with local stone and installed fireplace mantles made of Missouri marble shipped up from Carthage.

Molly's idea is to contrast the threatened loss of Route 66 Chapel with the continued existence of the Paterson family home. She'll try to say he wants to keep tradition alive when it serves his personal goals, but not the community's.

Still uncertain of her own logic, Molly saw Carl fall in with Claire at the front of the procession. She was pleased to find him here and not off at the Lake, but she wondered what had brought him back. It was a question his wife asked directly.

"I wanted to see what happens," Carl explained unconvincingly. "After all, you've gone to a lot of trouble."

"Why, thank you," Claire responded. "That's the first time you've been in the store since I finished the work. You like it?"

"I'll say this: it takes me back."

"To when you first came there? Or to when you were managing everything."

Carl shrugged. Either he wasn't sure or he didn't want to say. Claire remained puzzled, but willing to wait for more explanation. For now, she had her part to play in the Rally.

On the other side of Carl, Jenny Grey walked distractedly. Gene had stayed behind to clean up the catered goods, but he told her Taylor was missing again, the third time this week. Their friend was so weak they could envision him collapsing and dying anywhere. They've begged him to explain where he goes and why.

"I've learned something ... something important," Taylor had said, gathering strength at each pause to go on. "About ... my family history."

"Your history?" Jenny asked. "You said you're not from here. Have you met someone, a lost relative? A friend of the family?"

"You'll know ... soon ... enough."

At least each time he'd gone out, he returned in a couple of hours. Jenny figured she has as much chance of finding where Taylor was in the excursion to the Mayor's house as by searching for him randomly.

Norma, as usual keeping an eye on Jenny, saw an older couple who also appeared to be watching the Middleman's co-owner. They walked a dozen steps behind her. "Retired military," Norma thought immediately, noting the man's erect posture, trim haircut, and aura of command. He and the woman with him (wife?) tended to look away or down whenever Jenny's gaze moved in their direction.

On the other side of Norma, Harry had managed to strike up a conversation with Ms. Thomas. Because it's her job to deal with citizens, she listens tolerantly to this resident's theory on why we call one part of a shoe its "tongue." Naming a shoe's "heel" and "toe," he admitted, is easy to understand. "But it's not the shape of the tongue, you see. It's the function."

"Oh?" Ms. Thomas was trying to be polite but also wondering about the conversation between Molly and Max up ahead.

"People think they go where they want to. The feet just do what the brain tells them: 'walk here or walk there.'"

"Yes?" Her query filled a pause in Harry's talk, but she was slightly amused by this discussion of mind and body.

"Feet can take you to places you didn't know you wanted to be. They're like tongues; they express hidden desires. You've heard ... well, of course, being in politics!--you've heard the expression, 'Voting with your feet.'" Well, what I'm talking about is sort of a 'slip of the tongue.'"

"Um-hm."

Harry found his own tongue. "Well, my feet have brought me over to you for a reason. Would you like to go out sometime?" Now Harry's feet have stopped Marilyn Thomas in her tracks.

Molly, unaware of this odd exchange, thought she might have an answer to her own dilemma. But she had to respond to Max's inquiry first.

"Did your friend Norma ever get married?"

This seemed to have come out of nowhere. "Well, ... " Then, thinking she might be about to violate a confidence, she went on. "It's a sad story, a young man who died in Vietnam. I'd prefer not to talk about it."

She wondered why he has asked. Ever since he questioned the Patriot Act that day in the Heal-All, she'd been suspicious of this man. If her energy wasn't consumed by the RR66CC right now, she'd try to find out a bit more about him. Claire ought to help, given the way he monopolizes Carl's time.

The town needs an ordinance, a law, Molly now thought to herself, that would preserve the historic buildings, Fairfield's heritage. If Paterson offered up Route 66 Chapel while protecting his own home, he'd look self-serving.

Connection, she thought. All the old buildings in the community need to be linked together--on a walking tour, for instance. So, wherever Ozark Giraffe and Fairfield Prime remain, they must be protected. Historic Fairfield is about to be born!

Johnson's Department Store, the Chapel, the court house (a Union hospital in the Civil War, renovated and expanded five years ago), First Missouri Bank and its famous Thomas Hart Benton-esque mural depicting area history (painted by the famous artist's pupil), and the Stone Mansion, symbol of local identity.

Molly is finally on Missouri Street and one house away from the mayor's home. The van she expects is parked as planned across the street and one more house away. She is also pleased to see Mayor Paterson emerge from his front door, no doubt believing he can sway the crowd with the same rhetoric that has won him elections. He can reach them through their pocketbooks.

Because the protesters are walking toward the van, they don't see the letters painted on the vehicle's side, KAVE, or the slogans which identify it as the mobile unit for "They Say," the television station's investigative news program. When Molly waves, the van's doors swing open and a two-person crew carrying camera and sound equipment approaches the crowd. From the driver's side steps a strikingly tall, flamboyantly red-haired woman with a microphone in one fist.

Molly turns around to face the marchers coming up behind her. "Please welcome," she says loudly, "Fairfield native, former Miss Route 66, and now St. Louis television personality, Willa Rogers!"

IX. Alternate Realities

"Hello, people of Fairfield and Phipps County," announces the well-known television reporter. She faces the crowd from a spot on the Mayor's sidewalk. "I'm here to cover your story, this grass roots campaign to save the Stone Mansion from cruel destruction."

It would be hard to say whose mouth falls open more dramatically: Ms. Thomas's or the mayor's. (Both dropped chins are caught by a camera woman who stands to the side and behind Willa.) Most of the crowd, who were not in on Molly's scheme, are also startled to find themselves fighting now for the mayor's house as well as for Route 66 Chapel and Johnson's Department store. As far as anyone knew at this point, only the church has been threatened.

"What do ... " Willa says, her voice swelling to the signature motif of her program. "What do ... THEY SAY?"

She launches into a summary of events to date (shaped, to be sure, by Molly): local residents became aware of many property purchases by an unknown conglomerate; mayor and key town council members had apparently been plotting a real estate scheme that would forever change the nature of Fairfield; a group of citizens is now fighting to stop the loss of the town's heritage.

Ms. Thomas and Mayor Paterson exchange bewildered looks. Molly winks at Willa and grips Claire's hand. Norma studies a worried Jenny being watched by the military couple.

"What I want to do," Willa says, looking now directly into the camera, "is make sure the state of Missouri understands what unbridled development can do to an all-American small town. This beautiful home," she gestures behind her, "should be protected from unscrupulous out-of-state investors."

This event will come to mark Fairfield's entry into the Cyber Age. A town resembling but not identical to their own, Virtual Fairfield, will take digital shape in St. Louis area television sets and be accessible on computer screens worldwide.

Carl has wandered over to where Max is standing, and they chuckle together at the predicament the mayor finds himself in. Carl believes events are confirming his cynical view of the body politic, and Max finds himself increasingly sympathetic with the effort to save the chapel.

Willa turns to ask the mayor if he has any hope his home can be rescued from destruction. A flustered Matthew Paterson tries to assert that his house is not in danger, but the fact that he has kept secret the exact identity and goals of Farmtown,

Inc. makes it difficult to contradict "They Say." Why wouldn't these developers want his house as well as neighboring Route 66 Chapel? It's close enough to all the downtown property that's already owned by Farmtown.

If Paterson could walk the reporter and her audience back up to his house and have them knock on the wooden door and press their hands onto the stone facing, he could show them that the Stone Mansion is real, present, enduring. And he could promise to protect it from things so large and powerful as a wrecking ball, a bulldozer, a series of dynamite charges.

But he can't put his own hands on the house Willa's magic creates (her microphone is like a magician's wand), nor poke holes in a version that is made up of on and off electrical impulses. The genesis of this ethereal structure was the fertile minds of an energized RR66CC. And its final shape has been determined by software codes, media art, and electronic equipment so complex those who use it don't understand how it works.

However, the mayor's political experience does come to his aid. He recognizes that his best course will be to talk vaguely of "accommodation--har-um" and "har-um--cooperation." The best of the past will be preserved, he says, including the building passed down through three Paterson generations.

Town Council has been fully informed of the benefits of this innovative venture, he insists. The people will support Farmtown's initiative, he asserts, once they understand it more fully. And, he promises on the spur of the moment, a public hearing, in front of "They Say"'s cameras, if they wish to return, in two weeks' time in the town hall to answer all questions.

Claire, noticing Jenny's distracted look, decides to tell her about having seen her young friend Taylor pass by the front of Past Presents the other day. Norma has let her know that Jenny is eager for any clues to where he's been going or to where he might be at this moment. Claire pulls Jenny aside.

Ms. Thomas has been staggered by that odd invitation from Harry followed by the surprise assault on her boss. And this attack comes from a woman whose long, lean body rivals the town manager's. (Willa Rogers is, after all, a former beauty queen.) But finally, Ms. Thomas finds her tongue. She fabricates a meeting in fifteen minutes for the mayor. (That "They Say" girl isn't the only one who can generate an alternate reality!) She proposes to escort him off to the town hall.

Willa conducts a series of short interviews with random members of the crowd and turns finally to Molly, asking about her alternative to modernizing Fairfield. With the remnants of the Rally listening, Molly offers a clue to the RR66CC's scheme: to unify past and present rather than make a sharp divide between the two. They would allow some new construction but preserve a fixed number of existing downtown buildings. These sites would be designated "Historic Fairfield," linked together perhaps through a walking tour and promoted by brochures, highway signs, the Chamber of Commerce.

What this means is a kind of quota system, though Molly would never say that on camera (or even quite think it). This is the tack she discovered while marching, a better conclusion to her speech. We keep both the new and old; we embrace yesterday and tomorrow. Let the arms of God be great enough to enclose contradictory principles.

"But where does Taylor go?" Jenny asks Claire. "It can't be far, as weak as he is."

Dwayne, the student who has worked at the Middleman and who has been listening, interrupts. "Are you talking about the boy who is so sick?"

"Yes." Jenny is eager. "He's an old friend ... not a ... well, someone I went to school with. We're looking after him because he has no family."

"I think he's at the church, or at least I've seen him on that block. Route 66 Chapel, I guess it is."

Jenny has heard enough of the church's history to realize this makes a certain sense. Route 66 Chapel has been a sanctuary or place of retreat for many. Her friend, Molly, after all, arranged a secret meeting with her future husband there years ago to confess that she was more than a little bit pregnant.

Jenny asks Dwayne if he'll go with her right now. Norma has joined the group and volunteers to go, too. She wonders why Jenny doesn't go after Gene. She also notes that the military couple has disappeared.

Molly sees the rest of the crowd breaking up but knows her Rally has been successful. Her chief ally Claire goes with Carl, apparently to look more closely at what the old department store looks like after renovation. Molly believes this is a good thing, the couple sharing the same interest for a change. She feels again a pang of sorrow at her own widowhood.

She is approached by Max, who has another question about Norma. But first he tells her that he is impressed.

"I loved the way you took the mayor by surprise, speechless."

"He'd better have plenty to say at the press conference. Who is Horatio Radar and what is this Farmtown, Inc.?"

"You're right. Keep his feet to the fire. Get the answers." He pauses a moment reflectively. "Say, Molly, I'd like to ask one more thing about your friend Norma."

Molly remembers his earlier question and her worry that she had said too much in response. She thinks about the differences between memory and history, the things we remember as opposed to actual events. It's sometimes as great as the distance between the reality we experience and its representation by media figures like Willa Rogers. After all, it was only a few weeks ago that she herself revealed to a circle of close friends the truth about her engagement and marriage. She had told no one but Jerry and their families she was carrying a child.

"When her boyfriend or fiancé was killed ... " Usually comfortable talking with anyone, Max searches for the right words. "I don't mean to be indelicate. Please forgive me."

"Who do you mean?"

"Well, I'm sorry to wonder about Norma, but I have reasons, reasons I can't tell you right now." He takes a deep breath. "Is there any chance there was a child involved, that Norma might have given birth to a daughter when her sweetheart was overseas?"

X. An End

Taylor is stretched out asleep on a front row pew at Route 66 Chapel, but his breathing is shallow and his face pale. Jenny isn't able to rouse him and begins to panic. She knows he didn't ever want to be taken to the hospital.

Norma says decisively, "I'll find a phone and call Dr. Sanders." Frank had agreed to come ... at the end.

"Will you stay with me?" Jenny asked Dwayne. "Not that there's anything we can do but ... but pray."

"Shouldn't I go ... and get your husband?"

"Norma or Doctor Sanders will call him. And anyway he's ... " She didn't finish the sentence. "We're not exactly what you think."

Dwayne is puzzled. He's mature enough to know that he shouldn't have been letting himself be attracted to the baker's wife, pretty as she is and only a few years older. But he'd established a routine this semester that brought him to the Middleman at least once a day. And he was always pleased when she had time to chat with him.

Finally he says, "I don't want to be in the way. But I guess I can stay until someone else comes."

He sits across the aisle from where Taylor is lying. Jenny paces.

Before Norma and Dr. Sanders arrive, however, Max Bridges slips quietly into the back of the church.

At the end of the Rally, Molly had been so surprised at his question (could Norma have lost a child?) that she got flustered and abruptly ended their conversation. She knew she'd probably revealed more to him than she should have for a second time.

"A child? Oh, no ... unless ... " Then she looked about her as if she had things to gather up and said she really must be getting back to ... to the Johnson Department Store.

Her own experience--pregnancy, the quick marriage, the miscarriage, the deliberate confusion of dates--had always made her suspect a possible similar situation for others. Had Norma put on a lot of weight that first year out after graduation, after Robbie went off to college?

Max tried one more question as Molly looked down the sidewalk in the direction of Main Street. "Can you tell me about that beau she had in high school?

Molly shrugged, suggesting that it was so long ago she couldn't remember. But she knew she hadn't seen much of Norma that year after graduation, her first at college in Columbia. Her friend was always working long hours at the Knit and Fit Shop whenever Molly came home. But it was strange that Ms. Miller had let her have a week's vacation before summer. Oh, dear!

Molly had known who Robbie White was, of course, a varsity football player back then. His volunteering for the Army had won the town's praise, and his death enshrined him as a Fairfield hero, if a minor one. But if he and Norma had had a child together, Molly had no idea what happened to it. She had never even hinted of such a possibility.

"Do you know where Norma has gone?" Max said. Molly was uncertain, but called back that she might have overheard a discussion about going to Route 66 Chapel. That boy the Greys have been nursing had gone out on his own, sick as he is.

Max was thoughtful. "I'll look for her there."

"But please don't say anything … about what I've told you. I really shouldn't have … "

What a tangled web this is, thought Max as he walked. The end of one thread is the beginning of another. Actions initiated years ago bear fruit now. And that fruit is only seed for the events of tomorrow.

It's not just for individuals, but the whole community, too. Whatever Farmtown, Inc. might do, is it really unrelated to Fairfield's past and traditions? Probably not. Even in rebelling against the older generation, young people accept the terms of debate established by their parents.

He recalls Mrs. Hart of the No Class Cafe in Confluence, who said we're all determined by our place in the family. We fight it, of course, but our paths go forward within the framework of our earliest years.

He thinks also of Mrs. Evans, who told them about Confluence's big flood a century earlier. It didn't wipe out the whole town and force them to start fresh. It only destroyed certain wooden buildings, which were then replaced by brick. The basic shape of the town remained, though its two halves (north and south of the main street) looked more alike afterwards. The hills and the river underlay the growth of the community, directing the arrangement of whatever kind of people settled in the region.

Also rising in Max's memory is Penelope, his wife of less than a year; they were both very young. In her beginning was her end, a genetic flaw working out its tragic destiny. Her heart, so rich and true, stopped without warning. That attack's origin was hidden in the genes of her ancestors.

For the longest time, he took Penelope's decline as a sign of our original sin, humankind's fallen nature. In this version of Biblical history, God's plan was complete before Creation and required all that followed: the Fall, Christ's sacrifice, the Resurrection. And we, Adam and Eve's children, are working out the inevitable, the fates of sinners and saints.

Only recently has he been able to reshape the meaning of his loss. Penelope's lips around a piece of fruit did not, he realizes, tell of her weakness any more than his Adam's apple is a representation of his forefather's eating the forbidden fruit. These figures are elemental representations of highly complex forces in a a vast universe. In such a complex world, God's hand is invisible and unknowable, but in the end, he believes, it acts upon a principle of love.

How does he know this? He is not sure he can put it into words, but, miraculously, faith had been restored to him a decade after Penelope's death. And he found his role in the church.

The front doors of Route 66 Chapel are slightly open, and Max goes through them. He slides into the pew directly behind the three young people.

Jenny sits at Taylor's head, holding his hand, which, a moment ago, had covered his eyes. Still across the aisle is a clearly uncomfortable Dwayne, tongue-stud guy.

Taylor, dreamily awake, recognizes Max as a friend and raises his other hand. Perhaps, Jenny thinks, Max has been hearing the young man's story in the same way he listens to Carl on their walks.

"Will you hold my hand, too?" the boy asks. Max does.

After a minute of silence, Taylor, in a whisper addressed to the air, wonders, "What will happen next?" Max seems to understand that the boy is talking about his own death.

"When I was your age," the older man says softly, "I was told that there is this life and the afterlife, two completely different things. We all share being alive in the world, it was said, whether we're good or bad. But then, according to this view, there's one place in the hereafter for those who are good, and another for those who aren't."

Jenny looks concerned. She knows Taylor feels a lot of guilt, and she doesn't want him to think he's in danger of hell and eternal damnation.

Max goes on. "But I don't think that's so. In fact, I know it's not. Since all of us are partially good and partially bad, we get to go down the same path." He speaks softly, but with confidence. "Everyone goes to heaven. And those you care about or who have cared about you arrive at the same time you do."

Taylor smiles weakly. Jenny presses his hand.

"So I'll tell you what I think happens next." Max's voice is soothing; clearly, he's had to deal with such situations before.

"Just as Jenny is holding your hand here ... " He raises his eyes to Jenny, who squeezes Taylor's hand again. "Just as she's holding you in Route 66 Chapel, Fairfield, Missouri, this day in January, the year of our Lord, the moment you leave, she'll be holding you there, in heaven for eternity."

Taylor closes his eyes. It's hard to tell if he's still breathing.

Max leans a little bit closer. "One minute you're with us, and the next minute you're with us. You won't feel the difference. Of course, there will be no more pain there, no more sorrow, no regret. We'll all be home, your mother and your father."

Taylor's eyes flutter and his mouth opens. Jenny leans down to hear what he tries to say.

"My ... mother?"

"That's right. And she's happy the way you remember her when you were a child ... a baby in Salina ... ."

Max and Jenny feel Taylor's hands relax.

Volume IV: Now and Then
Chapter I: Rigidity

Harry sat on his upstairs landing contemplating his navel. Dry, free of rash, and modestly tanned, it might, he hopes, be taken for the bellybutton of a far younger man. But he suspects it won't be.

Still, in an attempt to challenge the sad fact of his body's aging, he imagined Marilyn Thomas exercising in the nude at the Phitness Phlatterer. She does sit-ups, hands clasped behind her neck, and he sees her washboard stomach ripple. Has his pulse quickened?

He fantasized that the town manager rolls onto her side and lifts one leg over and over, scissors style. (He watches from the back.) The sides of her thigh could be steel girders; her hips are carved in seasoned oak, glinting with a light coat of perspiration. Should he open his mouth wider for gasps?

She rolls onto her tummy and knocks off a series of push-ups, twenty-five with no pauses or rests between them. He can see her tense arms and shoulders, the straight line of her back swelling to the perfectly molded behind. Was it time to loosen clothing for the explosion of desire?

He stared down past his navel: nothing. He is not a young man. With a sigh he stood, tucked in his shirt, and fastened his pants. He went inside to begin another workday.

Could, he wondered, this absence of physical arousal be a sign of something else? Since the Rally Harry has begun to question the assumptions that had motivated him in recent months. Perhaps he never really wanted a romantic life after all. Instead, these odd physical urges might be an indirect expression of other needs. It's sort of an inverted Freudian analysis: sexual desire is the less important surface force, while beneath lie hidden, deeper motives--status, perhaps, or greed.

The town manager had been tactful but firm in declining his invitation to go out--so firm he knew he wouldn't make a second proposal. She has a long-distance relationship with a man in Tulsa. (He suspects, correctly, that this is not true.) But she claims to be grateful that he asked. In any case, with that avenue closed, Harry must re-center his existence.

His work apron on, he turned the Open/Closed sign on his door around and unlocked it. He was ready for business, though, as usual the sidewalk was empty in both directions.

When, still in school, he began to work for Mr. Manette, he had been thrilled to think how close to the heart of town this shop was. Up half a block to Main and he'd be at the center of Fairfield, if not at its geographic midpoint. And pedestrians were on the move on Eighth Street at all hours. But now the center has evaporated, spread out in every direction to shopping centers, new neighborhoods, the land of Full-Mart.

Post-Marilyn, his life ought to be a simple resumption of the routine that had satisfied him for forty years. It is certainly unlikely that another sweet young thing will appear on his horizon. He has been surprised to find, however, that picking up where he'd left off isn't as easy as he thought.

He took up a pair of cowboy boots that needed new heels and set to work.

It could just be that the excitement brought on by the Rally and the upcoming press conference with the mayor are upsetting Harry. He can't seem to slip out of his association with the RR66CC, so he knows he'll have to sit with the concerned citizens. He thinks the campaign doomed now, but clearing his mind of all the clutter might reveal the core of his true interests.

The Heal-All's door swung open. Carl Kendrick stepped in and placed an old leather wallet on the counter, saying, "Harry, I need to bring this old thing back to life."

Harry and Carl have known each other since boyhood, growing up on neighboring farms in a quiet part of the county. They would not call each other close friends, but they managed neighboring downtown businesses from the the 1960s into the next millennium.

"It's worn, and much of the thread has rotted out," said Harry, opening it to examine the separate sections. It's one of those large billfolds, folded like a book with a ring and chain at one corner. Traveling salesman, before the days of credit cards, would carry enough cash and receipts inside to buy and sell throughout an entire county.

Harry asked, "Are you sure it's worth it? You can get a new one, as I guess you know. And probably for not much more than you'd have to pay me."

Carl took it back for a minute and turned it over in his hands. "This billfold was my grandfather's. He gave it to my father, who passed it on to me. My boys aren't interested in having such a relic right now. But maybe one day they'll understand what it means."

"You want me to renew the leather? I can do that … well, for nothing extra."

"I don't want it to look like something brand new. It needs to show its age. See that scrape along here? And this notch where a piece is missing? There's a story for each mark."

"Well, then, I'll keep all that, just refresh it a bit. Sew everything together tight. Is there some reason you want this done?"

Harry gave a little chuckle. "It's something Claire ... she needs to know about it. Once I've told her, I may say something more about it. But, remember: this is important. Max said I should have it done."

Harry didn't see what Max would have to do with a Kendrick family heirloom, but he didn't mind this little piece of business, more interesting than most of the repairs he does. There's a sense of history in it.

When Carl was gone, Harry wished he could have more projects like fixing the old billfold, where the article is an expression of the past or maybe a gesture toward the future. If that happened more often at the Heal-All, resuming his celibate lifestyle would be easier.

Perhaps, though, he is contradicting himself. Does he really want stability, routine, a rigid order to daily life? Or is he secretly hoping for disturbances, outside forces that might prove catalysts to change?

Apparently there was a crisis coming on for that young couple around the corner, the Greys. He understood from Norma that her stiff military parents were demanding she return east with them, to what life he isn't sure. He doesn't feel as close to them as she does, but he does see that they're proud of the life they've built in Fairfield. If they leave, Norma will retire for sure.

He positioned the left boot on his wooden last, familiar podium for his thoughts. Although scarred by a thousand inadvertent strokes and stained by colorings, countless drops of glues, and even his own blood, the form would endure through another generation, if Harry had a successor. But he knows he'll be Fairfield's final shoemaker.

His mentor and first boss, Mr. Manette, taught him much of the shoemaking trade's tradition, which will disappear when Harry retires. In former days there were specialists for different tasks. "Clickers" measured the customer's feet, cut the leather, and assembled the final product. Dying and waxing the shoe was done by the "finisher." The upper leather was sewn together by a "closer." Harry regretted that he'd not lived in an era of clearly defined tasks, each with appropriately designed tools.

Molding the hard heel to the bottom of the current boot, he asked himself if maybe he shouldn't be looking into the option of retirement himself. He wouldn't want to leave the area, but if he sold his store for a good price, and then became eligible for Social Security, perhaps he could find a small place on the edge of town. It's another year and half until his 62nd birthday, but that could be just enough time to take care of all the details.

Again, he felt a pang that he would be the end of this line. When he first took over the business, he assumed boys like himself would knock on the door regularly and ask for work. He would train them just as Mr. Manette had taught him and finally select the one who loved shoe repair the most to inherit the Heal-All.

Did he ever think the next in the tradition of such men would be related, a son? He probably didn't, so convinced had he always been that he was destined to live alone. But he might have been like a son. Perhaps it would have been an orphan who needed a father figure. In time, of course, Harry came to terms with his quiet life, refining his lifestyle to be free of complications.

His shop door opened again. A man he will come to know as Horatio Radar entered. He was a large man in an expensive suit who surveyed the interior of the Heal-All more as if he were studying architecture than bringing leather work to Harry.

"Tell me something," he said without introducing himself. "Wouldn't this building make a fine stables?"

II. Family

If there were more room, Norma would be storming about in the Knit and Fit Shop. Those Greys were spoiling the reputation of parents in general, bothering Jenny so. She wished she had the space of Claire's new store to heave boxes in and kick the contents around a bit.

As it was, she had to stew in the tiny space at the back of the shop where her desk was. That's where Molly found her when she came to announce her second, recent discovery (the first was that Max thought Norma might have had a child with Robbie Burns).

"That Horatio Radar man is in town," Molly said with an appropriate sense of drama. "He's going to be at the press conference tomorrow."

"I know. He was here yesterday." Norma was moving stacks of yarn catalogs from the top of her desk and piling them on the floor. Some had spilled over, and none was particularly orderly.

Molly feels the surprise she meant to inspire in Norma. "He was here?"

"I've been so upset for Jenny that I forgot to tell you. He's behind the offer to buy my store." She waved a hand at her desk and at her life's work lining the shelves, filling the counters, hanging on racks. It might have been the gesture of someone giving up.

Molly implored her, "Oh. Oh, I hope you told him to go away. I mean, I know you have to do what's best for ... for ... " She couldn't finish her sentence.

The growing realization that the RR66CC might well collapse in the face of the forces arrayed against it was making Molly desperate. And here was another ally gone. She worries that Carl will distract Claire and that together they will concentrate on the new antique store.

Molly had found in the last year that she can't face just going to work every day without some greater cause to inspire her. Should she give up, too, and move to Sedalia? Her older son, who lives there with his wife and three children, has repeatedly stressed the advantages to a grandmother. But that chapel ... well, it *was* the heart of the community; it was a larger family she'd committed to.

Norma said, "I told him nothing would be final until ... until some things were settled." She sat down at her desk heavily. "And I can't leave town if Jenny and her husband need my help. It's just so sad, them being bullied by her parents. I ... I never raised any children myself, but I think I'm being a better mother to that poor child."

Norma didn't know exactly what the Greys senior were demanding, but she knew the young couple didn't want to comply. The strain of Taylor's death had been severe enough already, forcing them to close the Middleman for a week. And in that time her parents had besieged Jenny by phone.

After one horrendous, long argument in person, Jenny refused to let them into their apartment. But the mother and father, taking a room at the new Everywhere Motel near the Full-mart, appeared determined to settle in for a protracted campaign.

Molly asked, "Can I help you? Are you reorganizing?"

"I'm actually looking for something, something I haven't consulted for many years." She pulled open the desk's file drawer and thumbed through folders. "It's another sign of the times, isn't it, that families don't support each other? Those people should be happy to have such a sweet daughter. And she's done so well here, building up her own business."

The desk Norma sat at, an old-fashioned and massive roll-top affair, had been in Ms. Millers' family for generations. In a tearful moment, the kind old spinster had told her protégée she would watch from heaven as the young woman sat at it and kept the Knit and Fit.

Molly watched Norma search, but she was also moving around her own mental furniture as she did so. This whole save-the-chapel movement had started when she'd called her friends together to tell the story of her engagement to Jerry, the single most important event of her life. And he had proposed in Route 66 Chapel. The little church had come to stand in her mind for what inspires honesty and decency in people.

The group of friends listening to her confess that unplanned pregnancy had become her family after she lost Jerry. The younger people call them "support groups," but she preferred more old-fashioned terms. How do people live without families, she wondered.

That Max, for instance, wandering the country all alone. Surely, he has relatives somewhere. Norma has told her that he was wonderful at Taylor's passing, grandfatherly or like a pastor. And he read the Bible at the service. But Molly's still suspicious of his politics.

Family to church to neighborhood to town to state to nation--that's the direction she believes individual obligations go. The lines are clear and absolute. People make fun of the "nuclear family" now, but--heavens!--it's a model for social order.

And isn't that what's happened in this War of Terror business? The people who flew those airplanes, they left their homes and families to destroy another community. And now it was causing their own places to be attacked--in a just cause, of course. That Saddam is getting what he deserved for attacking America.

Ah, but all that's happening far away from Molly Smith, the widow living alone in tiny Fairfield, Missouri. Democracy in the Middle East, if we ever achieve it (and she's increasingly skeptical that such people will ever accept freedom), if we ever achieve it, that won't take away her loneliness.

She's told herself she'd never try to steal another man's husband. Her interest in Carl was for his own sake, and to keep Claire from losing him. But Carl's sliding away from his wife in retirement had made Molly think what kind of companion he was, or would be. And that led to the unexpected hope that she might somehow find a special friend for her old age.

On the one hand, she hates absolutes: single or married. On the other, she doesn't want to acknowledge all those new categories--unmarried mothers, absentee fathers, or, even more unsettling--(homosexual) partner.

Molly snapped back from her own worries to remember why she'd come to see Norma. It was not just to report that Mr. Radar was here, but to let her friend know that Max had been asking questions about her.

"Norma, you know what this save-the-chapel campaign has done for me? It's made me think about the old days, even about when we were in school together."

"Um-hm."

"We had the Vietnam war. Well, we didn't, but the boys did. They knew if they weren't going to college or married or something after graduation, they would be drafted."

Norma looked up from her desk, where she seemed to have found what she wanted, a yellowed envelope. "That's right. Some of those boys got real lucky, spent two years in Italy or Germany."

"Carl didn't get lucky, did he? Still, he never talks about it. I wonder if Mr. Grey, too--or Major? Colonel Grey?"

"Colonel."

"I guess he was one of those who stayed in, though he might not have been old enough to have served in Vietnam." She watched Norma carefully when she said this. But her friend was studying a letter she'd pulled out of the old envelope. There was handwriting on the back. Molly couldn't--and wouldn't--read what was written there.

She kept up with her thoughts. "We girls sure had it lucky back then, didn't we. Nowadays, if they have another draft, they'll have to go, too."

Norma, looking up, sighed. "I don't know anymore. I mean, we can't figure out who the enemy is, who we're supposed to fight. Back in our father's war, there wasn't any doubt--the Germans and the Japanese." Norma will admit that she has still an irrational fear of both peoples. They seem peaceful and democratic, but … but once a country has gone bad, in her mind, it stays bad.

Molly wants to go on about the current crisis, the worry that, with military recruiters not making their quotas, her grandson might one day be facing induction. But she doesn't.

"Norma," asked Molly after a pause. "Now I wouldn't ask this if we weren't such old friends. You'll have to forgive me."

"What?"

"I wouldn't bring this up at all, except … Well, it's unfortunate, but Max, he says … he wonders if … if you ever had a child. I know it sounds silly and all … "

She stops at the look on Norma's face, because it confirms instantly that Max had been right.

III. Vacuums

"When is an old thing an antique?" Carl asked Claire. He is surveying the few items she's bought in the past week, now stored on two large tables on one side of Past Presents.

"Well, it depends on the thing itself, of course. Cars are antique when they're twenty-five years old, but furniture, it's not so simple. You're not worried that I don't know what I'm doing, are you?

Claire was holding one of the Octopus's carriers, twisting open and closed the curved panel behind which contents are placed or removed (though right now this one was empty).

"Oh, no. I'm sort of wondering if we're not antiques, you and me. We belong to another era. Especially me as ... as veteran ... am I some relic taking up space who should move along to make room for others, I guess the Iraq War veterans?"

Claire stopped turning the cylinder door and looked up. Carl never talks about his military experience. She's always thought his years in the role of supply sergeant might have been preparation for managing her Daddy's store, but that experience is more a blank in his past than a piece of his personal history.

"We're not so old," she said. "Especially if we start up something new at this time of our lives, this store, for instance." She looks at the empty space which she hopes to fill with an old kitchen table and chair set she has crammed into her mini-van parked outside. "We don't have to disappear from the scene, just change with the times."

This optimistic vision of the future, a late mid-life transition to antique dealer, is clouded now by increasing evidence that downtown Fairfield is dying. If the Greys give in to Jenny's parents, and Norma goes ahead with her retirement, the chances of seeing streets full of strolling shoppers are less than ever. She asked, "Are you going to the press conference tomorrow?"

Carl followed with his eyes the Octopus tube above Claire's head, which cuts diagonally across the ceiling and through a wall into the office up front. He is one of the few who have sat at the heart of this delivery system. "I might. I don't really want to be at the lake right now. The house, without anyone else there, seems empty, so I might as well. And Max did say he thought it was going to be interesting."

"Does he know something about what's going to happen? Molly saw him talking with Ms. Thomas on the street the other day. He seemed pretty intense."

"Max says there's something fishy about this deal to make Farmtown the principle--if not the only--landowner in downtown. He's made some calls."

"Who is this Max, anyway?"

Carl seemed not to hear her. "Have I ever told you a secret about your Dad's Octopus?" The recently cleaned and polished tubes make the system stand out against the old tile ceiling. After the Rally, Claire had decided, it can be featured in a promotional campaign to draw people to the store and to downtown.

"Secret?" Carl was full of mystery today. She was happy to see him more involved in things, but was he more open with Max than with her?

"Yes. Here, give me that cartridge." She closed the cylinder panel and handed it to him. "Watch."

Carl held the cylinder upright in one hand and with the other twisted the rubber base that cushions its landing at a tube stop. It looked like he was unscrewing a jar lid. When it opened, he showed Claire that there was a hollow section inside the size of a tin of shoe polish.

She inspected it. "That's interesting. Do all the cylinders have that little cavity?"

"Every one. They were built that way, according to specifications provided by your father."

Claire rescrewed the lid and handed it back. "But why?"

"It was a place to hide a message in addition to the receipt, a box within a box. If we thought a customer was paying for one thing, but had another hidden in her clothes, we could alert the clerk. You know we had the two-way mirror?" He gestured toward the office.

"I knew about the mirrors, but not the extra space in the carriers. What would the manager tell the clerk?"

"All the clerks, when they were hired, were taught a little warning to give customers about the penalties for shoplifting and about the ways we had of catching them. The clerk, when alerted, would tell the customer that sometimes people just forgot they had tried something on and even mention the specific thing they were spotted hiding. It's remarkable how many times it worked."

"People would put back what they had been trying to steal?"

"That's right. They would say they had forgotten a hanger in the dressing room, or something like that, and disappear in there for long enough to leave what they were hiding." He seemed pleased to remember this little manager's trick. Then he asked, "Do you remember where we were on September 11?"

"Yes." She was surprised at this apparent change of topic, but added, "We were home, watching *For and Against,* just like we always do." *The For and Against Show* was a morning news/talk show on the Springfield channel. It was less professional, of course, than the network rivals, but the programing was effectively tailored to Midwestern conservative values.

"Right. Then we went to *Good Morning, America* and watched the second tower come down."

"That was awful. I didn't want to watch after I saw people … people jumping … falling down through the smoke."

"We watched the rest of the day, but, then, you know, we've never really talked about it. I don't mean we pretended it didn't happen; it just was too sad to talk about."

Claire heard something odd in Carl's voice. Was he coming down with a cold? She wanted to turn his attention back to Past Presents and to setting a specific date for the store's opening. But he went on.

"Here's something I probably never told you about what I saw in Vietnam." He took a deep breath. "You know I was stationed at a big base, Cam Rahn Bay, on the coast."

"I'm not sure you've ever told me. You know, I didn't meet you until you came back from there and started working at the store. And, of course, for awhile, you were just one of Daddy's workers." She stopped, but then added, afraid he might think she should have recognized his worth more quickly. "Of course, I saw pretty quickly that you were more than that. I mean, you were cute." She smiled.

He smiled back. "I had hidden depths." It's the first time he's made a joke like this in weeks. Then he was more serious. "Some things I kept buried pretty deep, even from myself."

Claire realized she couldn't derail this confession or whatever it was he seemed intent on making. He's not going to reveal something terrible about what he did over there? Surely there's no awful action he had to take?

"Cam Rahn Bay is a beautiful place. It's on the South China Sea. A great arc of coast swings out on the north side of the Bay, and from high points on the base you can look out across the water--oh, it's beautiful, clear, blue water--to that peninsula. We used to sit out in the evenings, when we were off duty, and just look at the scene, pretending not to know the enemy were hidden over there."

"Was there a beach on your side?" She'd like to keep the topic on the scenery.

"Oh, yes. White sand, and we could go swimming. There were lifeguards and everything. Of course, all the time we were doing these things artillery was firing, outgoing."

"You were under attack?"

"Oh, no. The enemy were miles away. We were just routinely shelling their suspected locations, certain grids and sections, squares on a map." He paused. "We blew up every living thing in some areas, but they never seemed to run out of troops, coming down that damn Ho Chi Minh Trail."

Claire didn't know what to say. And he continued. "You get used to the sound filling the air, loud as it is, day and night. There's no such thing as silence." Another pause. "And then there were rockets aimed at us every once in awhile, and mortar rounds. None ever landed close to me, fortunately." Another pause. "But, you know, when the alerts sounded, we all got into bunkers, concrete bunkers. And at night, you would see parts of the sky from there and wonder if something was flying out of the jungle across that sky, headed right for you. If it was, there wouldn't be a thing you could do. You were stuck in that bunker, just like those poor people in the Twin Towers. If someone looked out the window and saw that plane coming … "

IV. Public and Private

I told my daughter Jennifer, "Now, if Molly had known earlier how Carl was being visited by Vietnam memories, she would have been even more concerned about the future of the RR66CC."

"How so?" she asked. She and her daughter were visiting this time; the five-year-old was in the kitchen with her grandfather.

"Well, Carl was being drawn not only to the operation of Past Presents, but also to a counselor Claire had met when there was a high school class reunion a few years ago. And the biweekly drives to that service took Carl out of the scene."

"But this is when you enter this story, sort of long-distance?"

"I'm beginning to hear about things, from a number of different sources." Again, I'm trying to protect specific client confidentialities. "I didn't stay distanced forever, though. In fact, given my support of your dad's efforts to preserve Route 66, you might say I was already involved in historic preservation."

Jennifer laughed. "Oh Mom, you're going to launch into your favorite 'Don't ask for whom the bell tolls' speech, aren't you! I know, I know: it tolls for us all."

"Well, I didn't think it would be necessary for you, but I do believe we're all 'involved in mankind.' The death of an idea is a loss for everyone. And Route 66 Chapel is a powerful idea."

"OK. So, how did your joining the cause turn the tide?"

Of course, I knew that I was not the key agent in this affair; it was always a group effort. And the RR66CC's notoriety would soon bring other activists into the campaign.

I told Jennifer, "Not long after Carl recounted his bunker experience, she suggested he seek help. And she insisted the second time he awoke in a cold sweat and wouldn't tell her what he was dreaming. Not that she wasn't ready to do all she could, but she felt she'd be relieved if he at least consulted a professional. It's led recently, by the way, to his being involved in a veterans support group."

"So, coming in on the side of the chapel rescue team, we now have a television news personality and others. But from the way you've described this Ms. Thomas, I'm not sure their presence guaranteed an easy conquest of all villainy."

I knew she was baiting me a little here, but she was more right than she knew. Marilyn had not weighed in with all her guns. And if she had, it might have tipped the balance in favor of Farmtown, Inc. She was hard at work preparing her counterattack when Molly and Willa Rogers held a secret meeting at the Middleman Bakery on the morning of the press conference.

"The station's research staff hasn't turned up much about Farmtown, Inc.," Willa told her friend. They were in the bakery kitchen, having snuck in the back way because Mr. and Mrs. Grey were still in town trying to ambush their daughter.

Sipping the latte Jenny had set before her, the star of "They Say" explained further. "What they've found is that Farmtown is mighty elusive about its backers and its intentions. I think there was something to that Fargo operation, but we're told by an affiliate that the project never became operational."

"But what was that project?" asked Molly. "My insurance agent network only said it was some kind of agricultural idea. But Fairfield isn't a farm. If anything, the area's developing through the high tech businesses that have been brought in to work with the university or Fort Leonard Wood. In fact, we are turning into a vast educational-military-technical complex around here!" The allusion to Eisenhower's fear that a military-industrial complex was enveloping America wouldn't be missed by any of Molly's generation.

Gene came in from the front. He and Jenny hadn't decided whether they'd be able to continue with the store, but emptying out and cleaning up display cases would help them be ready to reopen or to move on to another venture.

"Is Norma coming?" he asked.

"She should be here with Harry any minute," answered Molly. "Carl and Claire said they'd be a little late."

Gene explained, "Norma wanted to talk about what we'll do after the rally. She seems to think we need her … "

Jenny interrupted him. "She's been so nice, but she can't help us out of the jam we've gotten ourselves in."

When Jenny didn't go on, but looked down at her shoes, Molly felt it wise to change the subject. "I probably shouldn't mention this, but have you noticed that Norma and Harry seem to be spending more and more time with each other? Not that the crusty old bachelor would ever get into a more formal relationship."

"Not all relationships have to be structured, Molly," observed Willa. She'd had an on-again off-again platonic affair with a married man for over a decade. A state representative, he wouldn't risk being turned out of office for divorcing a faithful, stay-at-home mother of four children.

Molly felt she was approaching another dead end and decided to draw the conversation back to the planned topic, their town meeting strategy. In the back of her mind, though, she found herself thinking of Max and his way of slipping into the lives of her friends. She was curious to know more about him, but no one in Fairfield could explain where he came from or who his people were. Many, though, were beginning to think he would play a role of some sort in this battle for the town's future.

If Molly hadn't felt the same way, she would have been suspicious of his taking out a trial membership at the Phitness Phlatterer. He would have just been another man infatuated with Ms. Thomas' athletic and erotically charged body. She believed now he was keeping his ears open to learn the mayor's plans.

Molly was momentarily sad, then, when the Kendricks, Harry, and Norma arrived and Max was not with them. All but Norma sat down to review the questions they would ask, dividing them within the group so that one wouldn't appear to hog the microphone. Jenny pulled her friend off to the side to talk with Gene.

"Norma," she said, "Gene and I think it's time we let you in on our secret."

"I might have to tell you one of my own," admitted the older woman with a gruff chuckle. Suddenly, she would like to confess what Max suspected about her because it might provide a reason why she cared so strongly for this young couple.

Gene picked up where Jenny had left off. "We didn't come to Fairfield to hide the truth from people like you, from all our new friends." He waved a hand at the group seated on the other side of the room, but the gesture took in many others. Jenny thought specifically of Dwayne as a special friend, though she knew Norma could understand that only after the larger confession they were about to make.

Norma said, "Maybe we all hide parts of ourselves, but most of us aren't honest enough to admit it." She nodded in Jenny's direction. "With the way your parents have been, I can understand your keeping quiet about family."

"We'd hoped to escape the pressure they were exerting," explained Gene. "We left college because they knew where we were, and the daily harassment was becoming intolerable."

"They're very patriotic," Jenny said apologetically. "And Daddy means well ... or he did initially. But ever since 9/11 he and Mother have felt all Americans have an obligation to join in the War on Terror. 'No innocent bystanders,' says Daddy. If his own children didn't join in in some way--and the military is his way--then he'd feel like a failure himself."

"But surely he knows there's more than one way to be a good citizen?" said Norma, unaware that she might be contradicting her own firmly held beliefs. To acknowledge multiple perspectives is close to saying you could have a third lane on Route 66, a two-way middle lane and not just east-and a westbound ones.

"He did at first. But now all the conflicts from his own past are driving him to madness."

"And to cruelty," added Gene.

Norma turned to him. "Can't you take her away? Sell out here and find another little, out-the-way place to begin again?"

"It's not that simple," Jenny said. "He found us because he has contacts in intelligence agencies. No, we have to confront him here, I'm afraid. We'll make our stand in Fairfield."

"I'll stand with you," said Norma with endearing determination "I can be pretty stubborn."

"We thank you most sincerely," said Gene, reaching out to touch her hand. He turned to Jenny and added ruefully. "I guess this is where we have to come out, right, Jenny?"

"Out?" asked Norma, who had only a vague sense of how that term is used by young people.

"Col. and Mrs. Grey are Gene's parents, too," said Jenny.

"But … ?" She can't begin to finish the question that had been building at Gene's odd use of the third-person plural.

V. The Public

"I'm pleased--har-um--pleased to have the public gathered in this fine hall today to hear about--har-um--about the opportunity our fair town of Fairfield enjoys. Enjoys--har-um--thanks to the collaborative relationship that your elected officials have established with Farmtown, Inc."

These words were, of course, grating to Molly and her friends, who believed they were "the public" and that Mayor Paterson was no more "pleased" to see them gathered here than they were pleased to have to attend.

Still, bunched together on the first row, they smiled to cover their personal resentment. A veteran of how public personas are created, Willa had reminded them that at any moment they might be on camera and their outward appearance needed to reflect propriety and sober concern.

"In a few moments," continued Mayor Matt Paterson, "I'll introduce to you Horatio Radar, the president and CEO of Farmtown Industries, Inc. But first, let me ask you a few questions."

"These will be rhetorical questions, I'm sure," Claire whispered to Norma. "We won't have a chance to answer." Norma was still in a state of shock over the Greys' revelations, but, for now, she was keeping it hidden, even from the others who had been at the Middleman that morning.

"Have we not seen," intoned the mayor. "Have we not seen--har-um--a growth of new businesses in Phipps County over the past ten years?" Everyone knew the answer was "yes," and the mayor paused for his audience to think that answer in private. Even Norma could not deny this assertion.

"But have we not also seen the closing of businesses,--har-um--the vacating of premises,--har-um--the flight of investment--har-um--from the once prosperous blocks of our own downtown?" Again, the gathering's inner answer must be the anticipated one, though a more open assessment, thought Claire, would acknowledge a new bakery and a new antiques store.

"So, isn't it clear to all of us--har-um--that steps must be taken, that steps must be taken to save our downtown and to keep the fair home of our ancestors--har-um--the home of our ancestors alive? We must have--har-um--an area that invites investment and development, a place so full of opportunity--har-um--that our sacred traditions and way of life can be preserved even unto the times of our children and their children."

This final flight of pompous verbiage was enough to make Molly scream. As agreed by the RR66CC, though, she too disguised her fury within a mask of focused interest. Her time would come to speak. And supposedly unbiased Willa should go first.

"Surely, Mr. Mayor," she said," you don't need to tell these people what's going on in their community. What they--and the viewers of "They Say"--want to hear is exactly what you and Farmtown, Inc. have been planning to do--to this point without a public hearing on the matter. Is it true that outside investors now own nearly three-fourths of downtown Fairfield?"

"It is, Ms. Rogers, it--har-um--is. But I am not afraid--har-um--of public forums. I am not afraid of outside investors who must, of course, conform to our laws, our tax codes, and our zoning restrictions. Indeed, I have called this very meeting to reinforce these principles--har-um--I have called the very meeting you are now attending and to which the media--har-um--have been specifically invited by my able fellow officer, town manager Ms. Thomas." He smiled at his ally, seated by his side.

"I was in the Middleman Bakery this morning, Mr. Paterson, and that little shop seems to me an example of the kind of new establishments associated with downtown revitalization in other cities, especially those with universities nearby."

The Mayor was prepared. "Ms. Rogers, you are--har-um--you are at least partially correct. The bakery has been a bright spot in an otherwise declining neighborhood, but I am--har-um--I am told that that small business is closing, the owners headed back to their native North Carolina." He looked pointedly at the ramrod straight form of the soldier seated stiffly at one end of the first row. Norma flinched at the gesture.

"Yes, we have had flickers of economic initiative by little--har-um--by little concerns now and then. But Farmtown, Inc. proposes to reshape, in a single grand design the entire fifteen-block area that is the center of our community."

There is an almost audible gasp from the crowd. Even those pledged to disguise their outrage have been unable to prevent surprise from registering on their faces. This momentary paralysis allows the mayor to signal to a man seated beside Colonel Grey, the same man who recently suggested Harry's Heal-All Shoe Repair would make a fine stable for horses.

"Friends and fellow citizens, let me turn the microphone over to a modern J. P. Morgan, a contemporary Henry Ford, and a present-day P. T. Bailey. I mean none other than the celebrated and accomplished Mr. Horatio Radar. He will explain to you the concept and the reality of Farmtown."

The newcomer rose and made the kind of sales pitch that had captured crowds of would-be believers in personal appearance, on television, and via the Internet. Those successes, however, had not involved investment--at least of money. What private self lay beneath the tailored clothes, a year-round tan, and a head of spectacularly black curly hair was known only to a select circle, which included Marilyn Thomas.

Over the next thirty minutes, the entrepreneur proposed bulldozing the remaining buildings on Main and its five crossing streets to create an agricultural theme park. It would be, he announced proudly, a variation on Massachusetts' Sturbridge Village and Virginia's Williamsburg, with participatory activities for all ages: tractor rides and sheep shearing for men, milking stalls and horse grooming for women, egg gathering and vegetable planting for the children.

"That means, my friends, jobs for you and for your children. Now," he cautions, "not in the construction phase, of course, as that will be done by our own contractors. But, later, we will need strong men to play farm laborers, attractive women to appear to manage farm kitchens, whole families to demonstrate weaving and pottery as cottage industries."

There was a crazy logic to the scheme. Increasingly, city kids grow up without understanding the processes that result in a McDonalds hamburger kept warm in a Styrofoam package. The relationship of the eye of a potato to a steaming hot French Fry would baffle many urban apartment dwellers. But Radar was also turning upside down ancient concepts of town and country.

"Rural and small-town America is dead and gone," asserted Radar. "Such relics are no longer vital to today's urban and suburban world. Entertainment is needed in the new age. Leisure time rather than property is the great commodity. And Farmtown, U.S.A., can entertain travelers from St. Louis and Kansas City, from Chicago to Tulsa, from Minneapolis to New Orleans."

Taken in the abstract, such a theme park might be educational and profitable, but razing the heart of Fairfield to build a mockery of its own past was, of course, unthinkable to the RR66CC. The outrageousness of the idea, sadly, was enough to explode their carefully planned sequence of questions.

Among the things Radar did not fully explain, of course, was that the scheme was to make Farmtown a model, not a working farm. The fields would sport astroturf wheat and corn. The kitchen canning processes were to be represented in plastic forms. The animals (and even most of the people) would be sophisticated, computerized robots, programmed to pull weeds, shuck corn, and put up preserves. Most of the tours would be self-guided, though the hands-on experience of the agricultural life would require living locals as something like tour guides. The real jobs, of course, would go to Farmtown's own hi-tech staff, lawyers, and accountants.

Norma snorted at the rural village idea: too many people around here openly live the nineteenth-century life Farmtown proposes to represent. There *are* hillbillies, and they're not going to drive into town to see their own backyards.

More savvy perhaps, Claire wondered unhappily if a referendum on the idea wouldn't pass in the county. After all, the folks who live in newer neighborhoods at the edge of town or beyond get everything they need at Full-mart. Why not devote the old downtown to an ambitious project that might generate revenue but not tax the county's infrastructure?

Only one observer from those who hoped to save Route 66 Chapel remained unflustered by Radar's presentation--Max Bridges. In fact, the little smile that grew in his expression along with the public relations images being created suggested he knew what Paterson and Radar were being careful to conceal. And perhaps he knew something even they did not suspect.

VI. Inside the Gender Divide

Norma had been so astounded at Jenny's revelation, back at the Middleman before the press conference, that she just sat frozen looking at her young friend. If the senior couple were Gene's parents, didn't that mean she and Jenny were brother and sister? Then the central RR66CC group had risen from their chairs across the room, the strategy session ended, and Norma rose mechanically to join them.

Jenny had put her hand on her old friend's arm and said, "We're not ... we're not brother and sister."

This was even more confusing. If not brother and sister, how could they both be children of the same parents? Maybe they were half-brother and sister, sharing the same father, but children of different mothers. But couldn't Gene, a man after all, defy his father and take Jenny away? That's what sons do, after all, isn't it, rebel against authority, particularly autocratic, overbearing men like the colonel?

Norma remembered a wrenching scene between Robbie and his father forty years ago. Mr. Burns had wanted his son to finish at the College of the Ozarks, then take a place with Burns' Hardware, an established Main Street business. But

Robbie caught patriotic fever and enlisted in the Marines to serve his country.

Like others in his generation, Robbie believed we had to stop the Red Tide of Communism before it reached the shores of the United States. East and West were total opposites, he thought, divided by the Iron Curtain. And no legitimate traffic could move across that border.

"Robbie," begged Norma, "you're needed here." She was still a teenager, but beginning to see herself as a future Cold War wife. Her husband would do his part in the development of American strength at home. Her prospective father-in-law agreed.

The three were walking along Kingshighway, once the pathway of Route 66 but being supplanted in that role by the three-lane bypass that Norma believed contradicted the natural order. The Burns home was another block west and one block north of Route 66 Chapel, and the father had proposed the stroll when Robbie was home for spring break.

"You're engaged to be married, you have a job waiting, why would you want to head off to foreign places? Let those who want to make the military a career leave their families and friends."

"That's not what you did, Pop," responded Robbie. And he was right. Mr. Burns had enlisted in the Navy at seventeen and served for the duration of World War II. Miraculously, he'd island-hopped from the Coral Sea to the

Philippines without suffering more than occasional seasickness.

"This family has done its duty, then. Let those who don't want to go to college leave for Korea or Vietnam or whatever." Mr. Burns wasn't even sure exactly where Southeast Asia was, but he felt strongly that his only child should live in Fairfield. "Your mother and I, son, we need you."

Norma remembered seeing the back of the old stone church across the graveyard. She didn't care where she was to be married, though she had thought more than once that this would be an ideal site. The Burns were members of Fairfield Presbyterian.

"Cuba had those missiles," said Robbie, "but they came from Russia, the Soviet Union. Those are the same guys that are causing the trouble all over. They have to be stopped."

Mr. Burns hoped a compromise with his son would be possible. "This country has lost a President at home. Couldn't you at least consider the National Guard or maybe the Coast Guard?"

That's when Robbie blew up, saying that his father was trying to keep him from being his own man. But he wasn't going to stay in this little town and be the junior partner of "Burns and Son Hardware" all his life. He stormed off across the graveyard, forcing Norma to trot after him awkwardly. A last look back had revealed Mr. Burns slumped over like a wilted plant.

In one way, of course, she was proud of her fiancé, football player and soon-to-be Marine. But something in the father's anguish told her Mr. Burns had learned things in his war he hoped Robbie would never have to face. Robbie's decision--honorable, to be sure--cost her, she still believes, her one real chance at happiness.

All the years since, when she was improving and refining the operation of the Knit and Fit Shop, she continued to feel the dull ache of what might have been. And the baby she'd had to give up. That child would be over forty now.

She'd read of adopted children, once they were full grown, searching out their biological parents. If she ever received a handwritten letter from an unknown address, her heart skipped a beat. Would this be such an inquiry? If it was, how would she react?

As she grew older, of course, the fear (or was it hope?) that she'd get that letter or telephone call lessened. But recently, the arrival of Jenny Grey in her life had brought back the tantalizing thought. She felt such an immediate liking (kinship?) for that child, could it be … ?

Now, Jenny's enigmatic statement that her parents were also Gene's parents allowed her to hold on to, if barely, the illogical fantasy of a living grandchild. If Jenny had been adopted, but Gene their natural child … Norma could only pray and wait.

The complete answers about the young couple's identities did not come until after the press conference. Like so many events in this story, the final revelations about Gene and Jenny came in Route 66 Chapel.

Molly asked the key figures in the campaign to meet there, perhaps for the last time, as the mayor's announcement and Radar's presentation had clearly weakened the RR66CC's resolve. She hoped inspiration would come to the group in the same way her boyfriend was moved to propose so many years ago in that church.

Carl came with Claire, which Molly saw as a good sign for their relationship as well as, perhaps, one more person drawn a bit more into the cause. Max slipped away right after the meeting but said to Molly he thought he had an idea that would help.

Before Molly could seek everyone's opinion, Jenny asked to speak. What she said put a stop to other considerations.

"Gene," Jenny said, "is really Genevieve."

This made no sense to the others. Then Gene/Genevieve stood up and ruffled her hair, which she'd always combed close to her head. It fell into a layered cut that a woman might wear. When she spoke her voice was markedly less rough and higher pitched than they had become used to.

"We're, um ... we're sisters. I'm not a man, but a woman dressed up as a man."

It still wouldn't sink in. A person everyone had known for more than a year as a husband was not only not married but not even male?

She (not he) continued. "When we decided to disappear from the world, to sort things out, we thought we might have a better chance of going undiscovered disguised as a couple. I was a drama major in college and, actually, had played women in Shakespeare plays who pretend to be men."

Jenny added, "She really is talented." But that hardly needed to be said, so effectively had she carried off this role. She didn't go on to explain that, in Shakespeare's day, no women were allowed on stage, so boys took all the feminine roles.

"I'm reasonable tall," added Genevieve. "And to take those parts I had to learn typically masculine gestures and stances. Too, many fashions today are sort of unisex, so I chose clothes that might be worn by men or women. And under an apron, who can tell? But you can also see that I stayed in the kitchen most of the time and let Jenny work the front."

Norma's mind was racing. Jenny *could* have a romantic interest in Dwayne, the student with the metal in his mouth. And Genevieve might well have been forced to leave someone back in North Carolina. Was Taylor more than a needy friend of both? And most importantly to Norma, were those two unpleasant military figures the biological parents of both of these girls?

Beneath those questions were also deeper worries. Suppose--and this had to be by far the most likely case--suppose she and Jenny were not related at all, what would she do then? Could she accept the offer for her shop, knowing full well that Radar and Farmtown, Inc. were behind it?

She thought of a plastic replica of a farm wife's spinning wheel where her old desk, the desk passed on to her by her mentor, Ms. Minnie Miller, still stood. In the letter she'd recently pulled from its depths was a plea to keep the business alive for future generations. And Minnie had been as good as a biological mother to Norma, teaching her the trade but treating her like her own daughter. Could the recipient of such love retire with a good conscience to Florida? No, of course not.

VII. Lies, but Fewer Lies

Molly might never had gotten back to the topic of saving Route 66 Chapel after Genevieve's revelation if it hadn't been for Max's entering the church. She was ready to give up the cause, at least for the day, but the big grin on his face was encouraging.

"Why are you smiling?" Carl asked Max, who knew more than the others what his friend had been looking into. "Good stuff on Radar and Farmtown?"

"Oh, the truth will set you free," laughed Max. "Free at least of worry about someone plowing up downtown Fairfield."

Norma, already made uneasy by one discovery of truth (Genevieve's sex), feared more revelation from Max. He seemed to know about her own past. Although Norma was ready in some ways to face having given up her baby for adoption, she preferred not to have the facts come out in this public forum.

She looked aside and saw her oldest acquaintance, Harry Blackburn. He would be the only other one who would know. He caught her eye and gave her, unexpectedly, a warm smile. Oh-oh, was he in on some plot to lay bare her private life?

Molly hoped Max's information would also show a hidden side to Ms. Thomas, that all-too-slim-and-fit reminder of her own aging. But she would settle for any way to preserve religion as the bedrock of this community, if not of civilization itself.

Max began, "The truth comes in two packages: Horatio Radar's own past and Farmtown, Inc.'s financial status. The man himself is an amusing, old-fashioned kind of impostor, and the business is a more sophisticated, contemporary version of corporate fraud. In both cases, when the rest of town finds out, I don't think the mayor, even with all his slippery political skills, can find the backing to pursue this scheme."

"How do you know these things?" asked Norma. "You're not a private detective or something, are you?"

"No," he laughed. "I once was a minister, but that was some years ago. Once I gave up that calling, I worked for many years as a research associate at a major university library. That's where I got the contacts I've used to unearth these stories."

"You were a minister, though?" asked Molly, obviously intrigued, perhaps even pleased, to learn this. It didn't negate her vague sense of his not being a proper patriot by disliking post-9/11 security practices, but one could concede that a man of God sometimes was required to resist secular authorities.

"Ordained, licensed, all the rights and duties thereof," he confirmed, looking pointedly at Molly. Then, turning to the whole crowd, he went on, "My story isn't all we need to focus on right now. Yes, we have to stop Paterson and his cronies, but I think we also have to find effective ways to promote Molly's alternative to an agricultural Disneyland constructed amid the rubble of Fairfield."

Claire asked, "Why are you so sure that we can stop Radar?"

"Well, to begin with, he's wanted by the government of South Africa--embezzlement and fraud. The man's basically a television evangelist, a phony who bilked thousands to bankroll his personal lifestyle--boats, resort homes, stylish cars. Your reporter friend probably didn't find out about him because he's only recently come to this country. And the red tape involved in seeking his extradition is considerable."

"And this business corporation, Farmtown, Inc.?"

"It once was a legitimate concern, developer of theme parks on a modest scale. But Radar has some accomplices who engineered an electronic acquisition by a larger group, apparently fictitious, with so many offshore accounts no one could tell who or what they really were. It was a reasonably clever operation, but two federal agencies are building a case that will eventually bring arrests and formal charges."

"Paterson," asked Molly. "The mayor and the town manager, are they in on it?"

"I doubt it. My guess is the mayor's been duped from the beginning. Now, Ms. Thomas, she's not quite all she seems either, but I don't think she's part of Radar's entourage."

"But she's part of something else?"

"She is, I think, a free agent. But I did overhear an embarrassing conversation she was having on her cell phone at the Phitness Phlatterer. I suspect she'll be leaving town of her own free will before very long."

Max chuckled at what he recalled, but he also remembered the not altogether unpleasant task he'd set for himself of spying on a woman with a polished outer mask and analogously sculpted body. His discovery was not, though, a happy one.

He noticed Molly raising her eyebrows, curious, he suspected, to hear the town manager's secrets. But, still a minister in his heart, he wouldn't be that unkind.

What he had overheard while using the treadmill behind Ms. Thomas (an effective distraction to his own legs' complaints during exertion) was her conversation with a plastic surgeon. He wondered at first why she had programmed her machine for a modest walk rather than a brisk run, but now he understood. She was reporting some odd sensations in her flat tummy and firm backside, a sense of shifting. Then she punched the "stop" button on the treadmill and listened intently. Parts of her body apparently were coming loose.

"Immediately?" she asked, clearly repeating the doctor's instructions. "More surgery now?"

When she stepped off the machine and reached for the towel on the bench beside her, Max saw that her face was pale, despite its cultivated tan. And she walked unsteadily toward the showers.

More involved than he'd been previously, Carl asked what the RR66CC should do now. "Do we confront these people? In the old days, we'd give the facts to Mr. Sweet at the *Mirror*, and we could get it on the front page by the end of the week."

Claire suggested they see what could be accomplished quietly, behind the scenes. Everyone agreed that Max, who had found Farmtown to be a house of cards, should deliver the news that would cause it to collapse.

"Will you meet with the mayor?" Molly asked. "Why, this will preserve more than Route 66 Chapel. When others realize the kind of people who want to take over their town, I bet we'll get a lot more support for Historic Fairfield."

Max agreed, but not without first offering to let another have that role or to be himself just one of a group. The opinion was unanimous: he was their spokesperson.

As everyone prepared to leave the chapel, he stepped over to Molly's side and said, "I'd like to get together with you in the next day or so."

"Of course. We'll need to be more specific about how Route 66 Chapel might figure in the town's future. And you are ... well, you *are* a minister ... and it *is* a church."

He smiled at the implication he might have a calling and said he'd talk about that, too. "But one more thing; I need to talk with Norma. And it's very private. Could you prepare her for my call. Explain that I have no wish to cause her pain, but I am the bearer of some sad news."

Molly agreed, convinced by recent events and this man's manner that he had no selfish or hurtful motives.

When everyone but Max and Molly had left the church, Harry fell into step with Norma. She sensed that it was intentional.

"You know, Norma," the shoe repairmen said, "I think I've come to some conclusions over the last few weeks."

"You did tell me you were going to ask someone out, didn't you?"

"I ... yes, I did say that. Then, well, I thought better of it, or at least better of asking that particular person."

Norma studied him. "Maybe you've come up with a way to save Route 66 Chapel, then?"

He gave a little chuckle. "I might have an idea about how it could be used more, at least once. And that would help. You know how everyone's been insisting they understand the true nature of Fairfield?" He gestured to the others walking their separate directions.

"Sure. After all that's come out, though, I'm not sure I know myself anymore."

"Of course, you do. You and I ... why, we've always been essential Fairfieldians. We grew up here, we built businesses here, we've have deep roots here."

"I guess you're right. Maybe that's why I probably wouldn't sell my shop to an out-of-towner, even if it was a legitimate offer."

He paused, but seemed happy with himself. "Would you accept another offer, Norma? Why don't you and I, the two of us, get married again? And if you say yes, why we can do it in this very place," he gestured behind them. "In Route 66 Chapel."

VIII. Classes

"We're not leaving," Jennifer told Molly when she stopped by the Middleman a few days after the press conference. "Even though I'm sure we've shocked some Fairfield people with our disguise, we hope enough will be forgiving to let us put it behind us."

Molly patted her arm, "I know I will, dear." But the older woman did wonder about others her age who would be put off by a woman dressing up as a man. They'd all heard strange tales that there were groups of such people parading around in bars and even having their own beauty contests. It was hard enough to see the girls always in pants; women should behave like ladies.

"What about your parents? Are they going to leave you alone now?"

Genevieve answered, "Apparently Max Bridges met with them again yesterday, for nearly four hours. And they've agreed to go back to North Carolina, at least for now."

"I wonder what he told them?" mused Molly aloud. She was still distracted by the practice of women acting like men--where might it end? Weren't there people who physically changed their sex? What did that involve? She didn't want to know.

Jenny explained what Max had offered their parents. "He said he would urge us to consider ways to help at Ft. Leonard Wood, as our part in the national campaign to fight terrorism. That appeared to have an effect, at least the appearance of compromise."

Her sister added, "Not that we feel the same way he does about what's called the 'War on Terror,' which seems to us to have been used as a political slogan. But we do know we should recognize the sacrifice part of our society is making. You know, this 'volunteer' Army represents a social divide in our country."

Molly's expression showed she didn't agree. Like most of her generation, she'd taken at face value government statements about terrorism, extremists, threats to freedom. She didn't think we could compromise with those who hate America.

Genevieve added, "We were lucky enough to go to college ourselves. Not that we didn't work to get there--all the tennis lessons of our youth and tournaments on Daddy's bases earned us scholarships. But we were on that team or in class 24/7."

Molly said "I know," but it took her a moment to interpret the phrase "24/7" as hours of the day and days of the week.

"And we had a good high school education and parental support," said Jenny. "But a lot of those in the military now had no real option toward a better life when they enlisted. Many kids our age joined to get the benefit of college tuition later."

Molly didn't quite believe this, having assumed all along that those people knew perfectly well what they were getting into when they signed up. Going to Afghanistan or wherever was to be expected. But she decided it would be better not to argue the point with these girls right now, especially as they were willing to continue in her Historic Fairfield scheme as proprietors of a developing downtown business.

In the last few days, she had worked with Claire and Carl to chart an official Historic District. The Chapel, Johnson's Department Store, the Heal-All Shoe Repair, and Norma's Knit 'n' Fit were the anchor buildings, but now Molly could count the Middleman as well.

Carl had found an aerial photo of downtown taken in the mid-1950s and used it to produce a black-and-white map of central blocks, marking these places (some of which still featured Fairfield Prime) in sharp black outlines as protected structures. A half-dozen additional sites were to be proposed, having formerly been occupied by businesses central to the town's founding and early growth. They were shaded gray. The rest of the central area was white, suggesting citizens would have to debate their inclusion or exclusion in this scheme.

Carl pointed out that it was ironic the mayor's home was white, given its status as one of the best examples of the town's distinctive style. But both women thought they should let the mayor keep his house to himself, since he was going lose face--and probably money he had invested--when Farmtown evaporated.

That event was more imminent than anyone would have believed forty-eight hours ago. Radar had left town, reportedly to "check with investors." But he wasn't expected to return now that Max had passed on to the town council a package of documents he'd received from friends (Friends, in fact, from the Quaker church).

"By this time Carl had seen a therapist several times," I explained to my daughter. "And he'd agreed, not just to keep seeking help, but to throw himself into his wife's antique store project. He clearly wasn't ready for retirement, as the leisure time gave him too much empty time."

Jennifer asked, "Did this take him back to his war experiences? That would scare me."

"Well, I don't know about that. But from what he told Claire, I suspect he had begun that difficult journey."

This was a lot for my Jennifer to take in, as she had heard the Route 66 Chapel history in fits and starts, on the phone and during her irregular visits to St. Louis. Given what she does in her scientific research, though, complex relationships are the norm in her world!

She asked, "What happened to Willa's big story for "They Say"? Had she put in all this effort for nothing, no scoop?"

"The big story broke overseas and had some minor follow-up here. Willa did get a piece that was incorporated by the network. But the former Miss Route 66 was happy enough to have played her part in the campaign to preserve Fairfield's history. The saddest person, of those I came to care about in all this, was Norma."

Again, Jennifer was silent, taking in the last bits of a long account. I could, of course, have given her a chance to tell one of her own stories, if I were educated enough to understand the biochemistry she does. She's working right now on pleiotropy, the study of proteins that have multiple effects.

I told her Norma's history. A month after Robbie shipped off to Southeast Asia, she found herself pregnant. She was willing to bear the shame that came in those days with her condition but worried terribly about her parents. It also meant losing her job; Miss Minnie was always most proper. But word came so quickly that Robbie was gone, she felt lost.

"How *did* a single woman in those days, a 'fallen woman,' I guess, find her way in polite society?" Jennifer asked.

"She had, it turns out, two knights in shining armor. One was Harry, the shoe smith."

"You're kidding!"

"Not a bit. I guess those two had known each other so long, even though they quarreled over little things, that Harry suspected her anxiety came from more than losing Robbie."

"Ah-ha! The young, soon-to-be confirmed bachelor proposed?"

"Not in a conventional sense. He suggested they get married in secret--by a Kansas City justice of the peace--and tell no one. A year later they were just as quietly divorced. But the child was legitimate."

"And no one in Fairfield ever knew?"

"Well, one other person did: Miss Minnie Miller."

"Oh! I assumed she'd be one of those to drive Norma out of town, or make her wear a scarlet letter."

"I must confess, I expected she'd at least ask her to leave the shop. But it's a little like the fruit flies and wing length you work on: sometimes there are more effects than expected from one cause, a single altered gene or a pair of altered genes. The world of human psychology is every bit as complex as cell biology."

I explained how the old spinster knew about Norma's condition weeks before her young worker ever thought about telling her. By the time her protégée confessed, expecting a righteous condemnation, Minnie had worked out a plan whereby Norma would work her last months in the back of the store, mostly out of sight. Never having married, never having had children, Miss Minnie was ahead of her time in thinking women shouldn't be ostracized for performing their most natural function."

Jennifer added that men are certainly involved in pregnancy ... well, at least until more recent times when all that's needed for some is sperm.

I went on. "Miss Minnie even used her life savings for Norma to take a two-week 'vacation'-- probably the longest time off of her career--when the time for delivery arrived."

"And Norma gave the baby up for adoption?"

"That's right, a girl. Until Max talked to her, she never knew if the child survived, where she lived, what sort of life she lived."

"And Max knew?"

"Yes. But that's where the sad part comes in."

IX. Faith

When Norma learned that Max wanted to speak with her, she invited him up to her small, sparse living room above the Knit and Fit. After a few of the usual pleasantries (which Norma expected, but in moderation), Max moved on to the subject of his visit.

He began with assurances that what he had to say was in confidence and would remain in confidence as long as she wished. Norma had already decided there was no reason, at this late stage of her life, to deny the truth if confronted with it.

"I want you to know that I learned, entirely by accident, about your past, about what happened when you first came to work here." He gestured downstairs.

She nodded. "That was long, long ago. Almost another life."

He went on softly. "I feel as if I've had another life too, as you say 'long ago.' I was once a minister. You may have heard that about me in connection with Taylor, the young man who passed away, the Greys' friend."

"Yes. They've had their trials, those two." Norma's sympathy had been deep enough to inspire eventual forgiveness for the deception they'd practiced as a couple.

Max went on, "I was just beginning my first ministry when... when a personal crisis caused me to take a temporary period of time off, then to offer an official resignation. Everything I'd believed in seemed to ... to fail."

"I'm sorry. As you know already, I've known loss in my time also."

"Molly told me about the boy you were intending to marry, the Marine who died."

"The Marine who was killed, yes." Norma was surprised to hear herself say this. But the legacy of Robbie's war--the only war America ever lost--had over time shaken even her Midwestern, conservative belief in an infallible United States.

"Well ... killed, yes." A pause. "So, later in my life, I became active in a Quaker fellowship. With Quakers, lay people have a lot of responsibility. I seemed to have some gifts for helping others who had suffered sadness, unexpected illnesses and death, personal tragedy."

At this point, Norma wondered if what he had to tell was not about the manner of Robbie's death. Maybe a comrade had revealed something terrible about wounds, pain. For a time, she herself had questioned the official version: "in the line of fire ... as a result of hostile action ... " Over the years since Vietnam, we've learned so much about "friendly fire," distant artillery or bombers targeting the wrong forces.

"I've seen that you are able to help," Norma admitted. "Carl has mentioned what a good friend you've been."

He smiled just a little. "Carl found a stranger easy to talk to, I guess. I can't do more than listen sometimes, but I can do that. Now he says he's going to get more trained help to steady himself for this new career in antiques. I believe you're going to have another Fairfield resident building up a downtown business, and one in the Historic District."

"You and Molly are working miracles."

"I wish I could work one for you. For you and Robbie's child."

Again she gave a deep sigh. So this was to be his revelation. She could hardly believe it would be that, in her advancing age, she might have a family, a son and grandchildren.

"Your daughter, Norma, lived a rich life until her twenty-third birthday. But then … "

The pause was telling.

"Then she died. She died quickly of cancer."

Norma, mother of a child she'd seen only at the time of delivery, could not stop a slow trickle of tears coming each cheek. She could say nothing.

"She did not suffer great pain," said Max. "Her one child, that story ... I'm sorry ... is also an unhappy one."

Norma raised her eyes, still swimming in tears; and he knew he should complete the last part of his mission as swiftly as possible.

"The child was raised by such strict parents-- unyielding really--who claimed the right to dictate every decision."

Norma could not stop her heart from leaping. Could it be ... those Greys, the parents ... was Jenny her granddaughter after all?

Max went on. "He went to the college of his parents' choosing and began the course of study they insisted on."

Norma thought, "*He? his?*"

"But that course was so wrong for him that he made a mess of his first year academically. And he got into drugs and other unsafe practices. When they learned that this had led to illness, to a fatal illness, they disowned him. Because he was legally of age, the terms of the original adoption were not violated. But, though he had always resented their iron rule, he had loved them in his way. And this was a final blow."

"Have I ... do I know this child?" Norma had found voice enough to ask.

"You did, in a way. This was Taylor, Jenny and Genevieve's friend."

It took a few more moments to sink in. "And ... and you didn't tell me until now. My grandson was here in town, upstairs at the Middleman, and I didn't know!" The tears had come again, and this time were partly from anger.

"Again, I can only say how sorry I am, but he insisted. He'd come back here, to see where his biological, his real mother might have lived ... if ... if things had been different."

"How did he know I was here? How did he know his mother was my child?"

"When he was first at college, away from his parents, he met a Quaker friend. He met me. I helped him find a government case worker, who contacted the adoption agency that had placed him. And he was allowed to find out about his mother's past, which meant *her* real mother."

"Did he come here to ... to spy on me? And I never even knew he existed?"

"No, he didn't come here. He read all about the town, in old copies of the *Mirror*. And there's a novelist who grew up here. In a series of tales--all of which Taylor read--she chronicles a lot of local history. He sent me a post card months ago saying what he'd learned, but not where he was. I thought he might show up here eventually, so I came to wait."

It was so much that Norma suddenly wailed, "How will I ever live now?" And she sobbed, her face in her hands, bending low.

Max was patient; in a few moments he began again. "I thought that myself at one time. I can't say what made me go on or what restored my faith in … in, well, life itself."

The need for any kind of hope was so evident in Norma's face that he went on.

"After a while, I went back to church, but mechanically. I read prayers and church documents of faith, not believing them at all, especially those passages about it raining on the just as well as the unjust. Why was I to suffer and others to be happy?"

"Eventually, though, references to God as creator, to this world as God's creation, translated in my peculiar mind to the simple conviction that something, after all, does animate the universe. It came into being; it continues to exist; we cannot truly conceive of the whole universe vanishing. Where would it go?"

He could see that this was not satisfactory, but also that she was listening.

"Finally, I reached the stage where I knew that whatever it is that's running the show, humankind often gives it the name of God. Joining in with the liturgy and ritual of any church tradition is uniting with others in the desire to understand God, this force that animates the world, that gives life. If I could feel that underlying, divine hand behind what happened even to me, I discovered I could go

288

on. I could wait for a better time to arrive. Which it did."

At least Norma's tears had stopped. And he had a final inspiration for the moment.

"I believe Molly has it right: churches--Route 66 Chapel very much so--represent the human effort to find God and understand God's world. I know this part is a bit heretical, but it doesn't matter very much to me what liturgy, what kind of service, what group of prayers--they all embody our desire to be connected. And we need to preserve the structures that have helped people feel that connection throughout the ages. They preserve ideas and values and hopes. Faith and despair are not opposites, but manifestations of the one human hope, one universal desire. Within them we are never alone."

X. Brides and Grooms

There was, of course, a lot more Norma was to learn about her child. Max did his best to pass on what Taylor had told him about her, as well as about the boy's own history, as much of it as he had been able to glean. Norma wasn't sure she had a right to their stories, after having given her daughter up at birth.

"One thing, I've learned," Max offered kindly, "is that we shouldn't try to resolve huge questions immediately. We're both old enough to wait for our hearts to guide us."

Norma couldn't say at this point if her heart would know how to guide her now as it had earlier in life. Her convictions had been so solid then--and, she felt, so just: only a fool would construct a three-lane Route 66 with its equivocal middle way.

She also would have said only a fool would propose to marry an old foe ("old" and a "foe") as Harry had done. He could not love her; she was sure of that. The confirmed bachelor ready for a wedding at sixty years of age? Preposterous!

On the other hand, some kind of marriage fever seemed to be sweeping through the community, affecting even old people like herself. Claire and Carl were going to have a ceremony in which they renewed their vows, with Max officiating, in Route 66 Chapel. The increasingly successful new venture, Past Presents ("Tentacles reaching from shore to shore") had brought them closer than ever. They were once again a legendary couple.

The old chapel, soon declared by Mayor Paterson the first "historic"--and therefore protected--building in Fairfield, was being cleaned and brightened, the grounds newly landscaped so that weddings, ecumenical services, and musical celebrations of holy days might be held there.

Matt Paterson was proving himself still an adept political juggler. Horatio Radar hadn't been a week out of town when his former partner experienced a sudden conversion to the cause of saving, and also reviving, downtown Fairfield.

In one more brilliant stroke, the mayor--soon to win yet another term of office--offered his own home as one more anchor building in the Historic Fairfield District. It would be open to visitors, he announced, on a regular basis, especially at town sponsored events. He offered the old carriage house as a visitor's center; its upstairs later became a modest museum/gift shop full of artifacts, postcards, and bumper stickers.

While neither Gene nor Genevieve succumbed that year to the marital fever, many saw romance budding for both sisters. Dwayne went to work full-time at the Middleman. And it was clear he enjoyed Jenny's company at the bakery and in their many after-hour outings. Norma smiled to think she might one day sponsor a bridal shower for her special young friend.

Genevieve was visited more than once, after their parents had left, by a former member of the men's tennis team where the two girls had been at college. And throughout these months the Middleman prospered by catering weddings (often at Route 66 Chapel) and town council affairs, as well as from the general upsurge in downtown shopping. The sisters also joined a volunteer group providing free baby-sitters down near Fort Leonard Wood for military spouses whose loved ones were overseas.

The greatest surprise for the downtown crowd, though, was the developing romance between Max and Molly, each of whom had lost a spouse. (Norma wondered if such a thing were really proper.)

Harry told the woman he himself had proposed to, "We're going to have to accept change. You say we can't change ourselves, but I'm beginning to suspect we're being made different by the times."

The two were at the Heal-All, he working quietly on an old purse of hers where the handle had pulled loose. He'd asked her to come by at the end of the day because he had something to show her. She hoped it would be her repaired purse, but feared he would offer new reasons to accept him as her husband.

"Can you spare half an hour for a little drive?" he asked. Cautiously she agreed, but told herself not to be taken in by his belatedly revealed charm.

Once they were in his mini van, though, Harry didn't talk of the two of them at all. Instead he asked, "I understand Max is not leaving town. Once he did such a good job helping to stop Farmtown, I expected him to go back to ... to his home."

"Molly told me some of his story," explained Norma. "Apparently, he had been a friend to Taylor somewhere in the East and came here to find him, not knowing exactly where he'd disappeared to. And he's comforting Jenny and Genevieve."

"But he came to Fairfield months before Taylor showed up."

"Molly says he came here for more than Taylor, but it's a sad story." Harry was not sure why her voice was unsteady, as if more than Max's history were involved. "Max lost a wife many years ago. I think they'd been married less than a year. But they visited here briefly and fell in love with the place."

Harry said nothing, but was pensive. He was driving across Interstate 44 (which replaced Route 66) north of town and was taking a small country road winding around the Ozark foothills past pretty, small farms and an occasional stand of trees.

Norma, clearing her throat, went on. "The young couple liked the area so much they used to talk afterwards--for those few months she lived--about settling down here. After her death he'd never been able to contemplate even passing through Fairfield. But a year or so ago, feeling the need for a break from his current situation--I don't know exactly what that was--he decided to come for a three-week stay. And he hoped that Taylor might come because the poor boy had talked so much about the town."

"He stayed longer than three weeks," observed Harry. He slowed on a curve and turned off on an old road, seldom used. Grass crew up in some cracks, but surprisingly few of them, sealed with forty-year old tar, made the ride bumpy.

Norma explained, "As Max got to know the people here--Carl, Molly, you--he learned the history of Route 66 Chapel. Gradually, he found he wanted to stay longer."

Harry slowed to a stop on the edge of the road and turned off the engine. "Hmm. I guess he went back to his past, to that point when he had ... where he once had hopes and plans for the future, plans he never got to see fulfilled."

Norma was silent. She had realized where she was. "This is that stupid road, isn't it? Three-lane Route 66!"

Harry must have thought what Max had done was more important than where they were, for he went on to say, "Max had assumed--like many our age--that love happens once in a lifetime, and with one person. There are no repeats, no second chances."

"Hmph," snorted Norma. "Well, we did always think there was a right thing to do and a wrong. Nowadays everyone seems to … " She was going to say "take a middle ground," but stopped. " … to … to not know what they should do."

Harry asked, "The main reason he's staying now is to see Molly, isn't it?"

"I think it is. I even think they might … I don't know, might become a couple eventually."

Harry looked through the windshield at the road in gathering twilight. There would be stars and a bright moon.

"I was sure I knew how I'd end my days," he said. "Just like you've said, since we were kids, I was destined to be a confirmed bachelor. I seemed to lack--I don't know--a romantic side."

Harry was thinking of what he'd believed was a late-life blooming of desire with Marilyn Thomas. Then he said, "Whatever I felt or didn't feel for a long time, for years, I've decided I'm ready for something else. I don't want to live alone."

He turned to the woman he'd known for fifty years or more. "We were married once, Norma, to give your child a legal name. I know we did it without the regular idea of love, but I have to confess there has always been friendship, even if it's been an odd friendship between us. And I wonder if that might be a better foundation to build a marriage on than ... than something else." He didn't want to say he didn't love her because perhaps he did.

For the second time in recent days tears unexpectedly filled Norma's eyes. Against all odds at her age, and seeming to contradict the kind of person she was, she was hearing a declaration of affection, an honest proposal of marriage.

She looked at the section of three-lane highway in front of her. She'd always thought of this as a contradiction, the collapse of values. But, though it ended now in darkening woods, she imagined it as one stage in a long and profound journey--unpaved one-lane country road, two-lane paved state highway, three-lane city bypass, four-lane country-crossing interstate.

She could not, at that moment, think where anything would lead her, but she understood that she and Harry could, in fact, travel there together. The proprietor of the Knit and Fit turned to look at Fairfield's last shoe repairman and smiled. "Yes," she said. "Yes, Harry. Yes."

Epilogue: Two-faced

At my summary of the current status of the save-the-chapel campaigners, my daughter Jennifer asked, "Does Dad know all this, the either/or dilemmas, the two- or three-lane highway question? He grew up in Fairfield, and he still goes back to visit."

"Clever girl!" I admitted. "He knows the basic events and is tickled that the old church has been preserved. But, as you are obviously aware, he sometimes is one of those 'Lady or the Tiger' people. If the chicken crosses the road, there can only be one reason." I won't tell her that sometimes these clear alternatives appeal even to me.

We were talking about Mark behind his back, so to speak, because he was out working at the Route 66 Museum west of St. Louis he'd helped establish. On some weekends and holidays, he sits at the information desk, not as a representative of the Missouri highway department, but to answer questions about the old television series or explain what Hoovervilles were.

Jennifer said, "I'll tell you what made me think of him in this context: the time he came to see you after Vietnam. Didn't he demand a 'now' or 'never' answer from you?"

I laughed, remembering it myself. But that memory has never been a simple one. His return from war was bittersweet, like too many of life's big events.

"He was ready to get married that very day and wanted an answer from me. I said he had to wait, but he claimed I was being two-faced." I chuckled again, knowing his earnestness was a product of an emotional homecoming, not a serious accusation of my character.

"I don't see you as a natural dissembler. Did he really believe you had led him on?"

"More tea?" I asked. If I was going to have to recount the experience, I wanted at least to stall a little bit before launching into it. She still had half a cup, and my own wasn't empty.

After pouring refills, I went on. "Before he left, I had insisted that we make no absolute commitment. This wasn't because I wanted to shop around during his absence. I felt he was the man for me well before he got orders for Vietnam."

"You were here in St. Louis, weren't you?"

"That's right, in my half of a tiny duplex near the University. I'd finished a year of my graduate program and was getting ready for a summer internship at Barnes Hospital. In many ways, this time marked a new phase in life for me, too."

"You were betwixt and between, though, not just a student, but not fully in the working world."

"That's one way of seeing it." She's the daughter of her father in this respect, I thought: you can't be both in school and in the workplace. "I guess your father was no longer a soldier, but not really a civilian again either."

"He's always said he had trouble adapting to the military way of things. Doesn't he love the saying, 'Something bad is to something good as military music is to music?"

"He did for years, but recently he's been rethinking what happened to him in those years. You recall how we made a pilgrimage to Washington, D.C., a year ago. He went to touch the wall and remember friends."

"But when he first came back?"

"When he first came back, he wanted to insist he'd never been gone, that we could pick up right where we left off." I stopped to recall that time more carefully.

While we had written regularly, letters don't tell the full story. Now, soldiers away from home can e-mail or use cell phones, even teleconference. The internet has almost erased the difference between *here* and *there*.

"As much as I had missed your father," I told Jennifer, "I worried that we might have drifted apart. And he *had* changed, even if it's taken him many years to accept it."

Mark at that time was like Norma, sensing, when he returned from Southeast Asia, that things had gone wrong in the sixties. He never referred to two- or three- or four-lane Route 66, but he felt he'd left this country at a crucial juncture. There had been a distinct break between the past and the present. America went, Mark felt, from confident Super Power to confused and powerless giant.

I couldn't convince him it was the same country in two phases, and that maybe this next phase would be a better one. There was a before and an after, yes, but also a continuation of strengths and weakness that had been parts of our national history from the beginning.

That silly story Mark tells about our son's birth--the one with which I started this account of Route 66 Chapel--illustrates his view of things all too clearly. He was either a husband or a father, not both. And he's had trouble leaving off this belief in dichotomies, in warring opposites. Warring opposites! That's exactly what he was struggling with more than thirty years ago. And, of course, I was, too.

Jennifer reminded me that I was supposed to be telling her the full story of her father's return from war. "Wasn't he carrying an engagement ring?"

"He rang the doorbell with the ring in one fist," I wiggled the fingers of my left hand, "and flowers in the other. He felt he should get an answer the moment I saw him--yes or no."

"Was he in his uniform?"

"Oh, no. He was back in one of the same outfits he'd worn as an engineering student. He'd left all his Army clothes with his parents in Fairfield."

"But you expected him? You knew who he was the moment you opened the door?"

"Yes, but, at the same time, I didn't recognize him."

"The change was so great?"

I could see more worry than I'd expected on Jennifer's face. Then I realized I was talking about her father, a father who'd always been a caring, quiet, restrained man. Even when he and our son were not communicating (Nelson had been a mildly rebellious teenage male), Mark has always been awed by his daughter's many talents.

The last thing any child wants to learn is that the image of a good parent is a facade, a hoax perpetuated on a willing and naive child. But we all discover eventually the flaws that make parents less than perfect. I tell my students who come for counseling (too often a child's college years are a time when couples divorce) that they will find their parents both better and worse than they believed growing up.

Of course, I hadn't been frozen in place during the year Mark was in Vietnam. My commitment to a professional career deepened, and I struggled with my feelings about the war. Interestingly, however, even as I studied human psychology, I hid from myself many of the the changes that self-assessment was generating. Still, Jennifer's question right now was about her father.

I asked Jennifer, "Has he ever shown you pictures of what he looked like in Vietnam?"

"He was thumbing through some photos not too long ago while I was here, but I don't know that I saw any from the war."

I was at a point when I could explain in two ways why her father was not the man who'd kissed me goodbye a year earlier, swearing fidelity and vowing to return. She was old enough I couldn't take only the easy route.

"Honey, your dad had seen death. He had seen it more than once, of those we called enemies and those he knew as friends. And that changes a person. I could see it instantly in his face, although … " I paused. " … although I never told him."

Jennifer was silent. I knew she wouldn't want to hear this; but I also knew she had learned in her own life. She, in fact, had lost a close friend through childhood leukemia.

Mark had lost three of his grandparents and a high school friend in a car accident before he even went to college. But war deaths can be more devastating in their number and manner.

Still, in order to end a story that began with birth--my son's entry into the world--with something other than death, I will add the same little postscript that I tacked on to this account for Jennifer.

"Your dad had grown a mustache while he was in Vietnam, very trim, very regulation. But I'd never seen him with one."

"So, you were shocked?"

"If I hadn't been expecting him, I might not have known who it was. But I'm proud to say I rallied. I rallied by subscribing to one of those either/or oppositions he loves."

She raised her eyebrows.

"I threw my arms around him, laughed, and said, 'Kissing a man without a mustache is like eating an egg without salt.'"

The End

Route 66 books by Michael Lund

Growing Up on Route 66 — Michael Lund (2000) ISBN 1-888725-31-1 Novel evoking fond memories of what it was like to grow up alongside "America's Highway" in 20th Century Missouri. (Trade paperback) 5x8 260 pp,

Route 66 Kids — Michael Lund (2002) ISBN 1-888725-70-2 Sequel to *Growing Up on Route 66*, continuing memories of what it was like to grow up alongside "America's Highway" in 20th Century Missouri. (Trade paperback) 5x8 270 pp,

A Left-hander on Route 66--Michael Lund (2003) ISBN 1-888725-88-5. Twenty years after the fact, left-hander Hugh Noone appeals a wrongful conviction that detoured him from "America's Main Street" and put him in jail. But revealing the details of the past and effecting a resolution of his case mean a dramatic rearrangement of his world, including troubled relationships with three women: Linda Roy, Patty Simpson, and Karen Murphy. (Trade paperback) 5x8 270 pp,

Route 66 Spring-- Michael Lund (2004) ISBN: 1-888725-98-2. The lives of four young Missourians are changed when a bottle comes to the surface of one of the state's many natural springs. Inside is a letter written by a girl a dozen years after the end of the Civil War. Lucy Rivers Johns ' epistle contains a sad story of family failure and a powerful plea for help. This message from the last century crystallizes the individual frustrations of Janet Masters, Freddy Sills, Louis Clark, and Roberta Green, another group of Route 66 kids. Their response to the past charts a bold path into the future, a path inspired by the Mother Road itself. (Trade paperback) 5x8 270 pp,

Miss Route 66--Michael Lund (2004) ISBN 1-888725-96-6. In the fourth novel of Michael Lund's Route 66 Novel Series, Susan Bell tells the story of her candidacy in Fairfield, Missouri's annual beauty contest. Now married and with teenage children in St. Louis, she recounts her youthful adventure in this small town along "America's Highway."   At the same time, she plans a return to Fairfield in order to right injustices she feels were done to some young contestants in the Miss Route 66 Pageant. (Trade paperback) 5½ X8¼, 260 pp,
   Audiobook on 5 CD's ISBN 1-888725-12-5

Route 66 to Vietnam Michael Lund (2004) ISBN 1-59630-000-0 This novel takes characters from earlier works in the Route 66 Novel Series farther west than Los Angeles, official destination of the famous highway, Route 66. Mark Landon and Billy Rhodes find the values they grew up on challenged by America's role in Southeast Asia. But elements of their upbringing represented by the Mother Road also sustain them in ways they could never have anticipated. . (Trade paperback) 5½ X8¼, 270 pp,

AudioBook on CD — Route 66 to Vietnam ISBN: 1-59630-011-6 Michael Lund's fictional commentary from the viewpoint of a draftee. by Michael Lund unabridged 6 CD's --9 hours running time.

Route 66 Chapel Michael Lund (2006) ISBN 1-59630-012-4 Route 66 Chapel, Michael Lund (2006) (Trade paperback) 5½ X8¼, 260 pp, When the forces of progress threaten the foundation of smalltown life — a small church — five senior citizens, a mysterious newcomer, and one young couple band together in an unlikely campaign to save it. The embattled meeting point of old and new is Route 66 Chapel, a building curiously linked to America's "Mother Road."

Route 66 Choir-- A Comedy (2010)

Michael Lund ISBN 9781596300583   284 pp 5" x 8"   In Route 66 Choir Stanley Measure takes early retirement just before September 11, 2001, and his impulsive decisions participate in an unraveling of confidence in the American way of life. His wife Felicia finds that everything she holds dear is in danger of coming apart: her marriage, her church, her business, and even her country. Who or what can orchestrate the recovery of harmony necessary to sustain the spirit of the Mother Road?

Route 66 Bride (Fall 2010)

Educators Discount Policy

To encourage use of our books for education, educators can purchase three or more books (mixed titles) on our standard discount schedule for resellers. See **sciencehumanitiespress.com/** for more detail or call Science & Humanities Press, PO Box 7151, Chesterfield MO 63006-7151 636-394-4950

Order Form

Item	Eac	Quantity	Amount
Missouri (only) sales tax .6.925%			
Priority Shipping			$5.00
	Tot		

Name

Address

BeachHouse
Books

www.beachhousebooks.com

an Imprint of
Science & Humanities Press
PO Box 7151
Chesterfield, MO 63006-7151
(636) 394-4950